Praise for *Tru & Nelle*

"Wonderfully imaginative . . . affirms the mysterious and glorious ways that friendship reaches across boundaries of all sorts to claim unexpected kinship."

—Gary D. Schmidt, author of Newbery Honor books *Lizzie Bright and the Buckminster Boy* and *The Wednesday Wars*

"[*Tru and Nelle*] reads like a classic. Middle-grade readers will be touched by their resilience in the face of dark family and societal situations."

—*San Francisco Book Review*

"A delightful tale . . . *Tru & Nelle* will enchant younger readers."

—*BookPage*

"There is a gentle, azalea-scented goodness to *Tru & Nelle* that young readers may fall for, and which grants space to the racial ugliness of the past without dwelling exclusively on it."

—*USA Today*

"A love letter to two cultural icons. . . . Neri's homage envisions a deep, rewarding relationship between two children before the literary world knew their names."

—*Horn Book*

"I think it's a valuable read for your kid, especially in today's climate. . . . It's also a funny, sweet, and heartbreaking read wrapped in a detective story. This is a good one that works on a lot of levels. Read it with your kids."

—Michael Buckley, author of *The Sisters Grimm* and *N.E.R.D.S.*

"Heartwarming, funny, and beautifully crafted; readers will be sucked in from the very first chapter."

—*School Library Journal*

Tru & Nelle

A Novel by G. Neri

Based on the real-life friendship of Truman Capote and Nelle Harper Lee

HOUGHTON MIFFLIN HARCOURT
Boston   New York

The text of this book is set in Adobe Caslon Pro.

The Library of Congress has cataloged the hardcover edition as follows:
Neri, Greg.
Tru and Nelle / written by G. Neri.
p. cm.
Based on the real-life friendship of Truman Capote and Nelle Harper Lee.
Summary: In their small town of Monroeville, Alabama, in 1930, misfits
Tru and Nelle strike up a friendship and find a mystery to solve when someone
breaks into the drugstore and steals some candy and a fancy brooch.
1. Capote, Truman, 1924–1984—Juvenile fiction. 2. Lee, Harper—Juvenile
fiction. [1. Capote, Truman, 1924–1984—Fiction. 2. Lee, Harper—Fiction.
3. Friendship—Fiction. 4. Mystery and detective stories. 5. Monroeville
Ala—History—20th century—Fiction.] I. Title.
PZ7.N4377478Tr 2016
[Fic—dc23
2015012612

ISBN: 978-0-544-69960-1 hardcover
ISBN: 978-1-328-74095-3 paperback

Manufactured in the United States of America
DOC 10 9 8 7 6 5 4 3 2 1
4500663767

PHOTO CREDITS

Page 318: Truman, age eight. (Photographer unknown, permission
given by The Truman Capote Literary Trust. Photo from
The Truman Capote papers at the NYPL Archives.)

Nelle Harper Lee, 1948 Corolla Yearbook. (Photographer unknown,
permission given by The W. S. Hoole Special Collections Library,
The University of Alabama.)

Page 320: Nelle Harper Lee and Truman Capote fixing plates
in the Deweys' kitchen, 1960. (Photographer unknown, permission
given by The Truman Capote Literary Trust. Photo from
The Truman Capote Papers at the NYPL Archives.)

For Edward

Contents

Art is a lie that tells the truth.
         —*Picasso*

I

1

A Case of Mistaken Identity

Monroeville, Alabama — Summer,
sometime in the Great Depression

When Truman first spotted Nelle, he thought she was a boy. She was watching him like a cat, perched on a crooked stone wall that separated their rambling wood homes. Barefoot and dressed in overalls with a boyish haircut, Nelle looked to be about his age, but it was hard for Truman to tell — he was trying to avoid her stare by pretending to read his book.

"Hey, you," she finally said.

Truman gazed up from the pages. He was sitting quietly on a wicker chair on the side porch of his cousins' house, dressed in a little white sailor suit.

"Are you . . . talking to me?" he said in a high wispy voice.

"Come here," she commanded.

Truman pulled on his cowlick and glanced across the porch to the kitchen window. Inside, Sook, his ancient second cousin (thrice removed), was prepping her secret dropsy medicine for curing rheumatism. Sook normally kept a close eye on Truman, but at that moment, she was humming a song in her head, lost in thought.

Truman stepped off the porch because he was curious about who this little boy was. He'd made no friends since arriving at his cousins' house two weeks ago. It was early summer and he yearned to play with the boys he saw making their way to the swimming hole. So he straightened his little white suit and wandered slowly past the trellises of wisteria vines and japonica flowers until he came upon the stone wall.

Truman was taken aback. He scrunched up his face; he'd been confused by Nelle's short hair and overalls. "You're a . . . girl?"

Nelle stared back at him even harder. Truman's high voice, white-blond hair, and sailor outfit had thrown her for a loop too. "You're a *boy?*" she asked, incredulous.

"Well, of course, silly."

"Hmph." Nelle jumped off the wall and landed in front of him — she stood a head taller. "How old are you?" she asked.

"Seven."

"You smell funny," she said, matter of fact.

He sniffed his wrist while keeping his eyes glued on her. "That's from a scented soap my mother brought me from New Orleans. How old are *you?*"

"Six." She stared at the top of his head then put her hand on it, mashing down his cowlick. "How come you're such a shrimp?"

Truman pushed her hand away. "I don't know . . . How come you're so . . . ugly?"

Nelle shoved him and his book into the dirt.

"Hey!" he cried, his face bright red. His precious outfit was now dirty. Seething, he jutted out his lower jaw (with two front teeth missing) and scowled at her. "You shouldn'ta done that."

She grinned. "You look just like one of them bulldogs the sheriff keeps."

He pulled his jaw back in. "And you look like—"

"Just what on earth are you wearing?" she asked, cutting him off.

It should have been obvious to her that he was wearing his Sunday best—an all-white sailor suit with matching shoes. "A person should always look their best, my mother says," he huffed, scrambling to his feet.

She giggled. "Was your mother an admiral?"

She glanced at the discarded book on the ground and started poking at it with her bare foot till she could see its title—*The Adventure of the Dancing Men: A Sherlock Holmes Mystery.*

"You can read?" she asked.

Truman crossed his arms. "Of course I can read. And I can write too. My teachers don't like me because I make the other kids look stupid."

"Cain't make me look stupid," she said, snatching the book off the ground and scanning its back cover. "I can read too, and I'm only in first grade."

With that, she turned and climbed back up the wall.

"Hey, my book!" he protested. "I didn't say you could take it!"

She stopped and considered Truman until something behind him caught her attention—Sook was fanning smoke out the kitchen window. Nelle squinted at Sook, then back at him. "Say, Miss Sook ain't your mama—she's way too old. And I know her brother, Bud, ain't your pa neither. Where your folks at?"

Truman looked back at the house. "She's my older cousin on my mother's side," he said. "So's Bud and Jenny and Callie too."

"I always thought it strange that none of 'em ever got married or nothin'," said Nelle, watching Sook. "And now they're still all living together just like they did when they was kids—even though they're as old as my granny."

"That's Cousin Jenny's doing. She's the boss of all of us, what with running the hat store and the house at the same time—she makes sure we all stay family."

"Well, why do *you* live here?" she asked.

"I'm just staying here for the time being. My daddy's off making his fortune. He's a . . . *entre-pren-oor*, he calls it. I was working with him on the steamboats that go up and down the Mississippi, but then the captain told me I had to leave. So Sook and them are watching me for now."

"Why'd they kick you off a steamboat?"

"Because . . ." He weighed his words carefully. "Because I was making too much money," he said finally, fiddling with his oversize collar. "See, my daddy brought me onboard to be the entertainment. I used to tap-dance while this colored guy, Satchmo Armstrong, played the trumpet. People were throwing so much money at me, the captain got mad and told me I had to git!"

Nelle seemed skeptical. "You're lying. Let's see you dance, then."

Truman looked at the soft dirt he was standing on. "I can't here. You need a wood floor to tap on. And besides, I don't have on my dance shoes."

Nelle stared at his clothes. "Who gave you them funny clothes anyways?" she asked.

"My mama bought them in New Orleans. That's where we come from."

No boys she knew ever wore anything like that. "Well, they sure do dress funny down there in *New Or-leeeens*. Is that where your mama's at now?" she asked.

Truman stared at his feet. "Maybe."

"Maybe? Well, for land's sake, why ain't you staying with her then?" she asked.

Truman shrugged. He didn't want to talk about it.

"Suit yourself," said Nelle. "Say, what's your name anyways?"

"Truman. What's yours?"

"I'm Nelle. Nelle is Ellen spelt backwards. That's my granny's name. You got a middle name?"

Truman blushed. "Maybe. What's yours?"

"Harper. What's yours?"

Truman's face turned even redder. "Um . . . Streckfus," he said, embarrassed.

Nelle looked mystified, so Truman explained. "My daddy named me after the company he worked for—the Streckfus Steamship Company."

Nelle choked back a laugh. "Well, I guess you wasn't kidding about that boat." She was going to say something else but changed her mind. "Okay, then, see ya 'round."

She jumped off the wall onto the other side.

"Hey! What about my book?" he yelled after her.

She was already running back to her house. "You'll get it when I'm good 'n' done with it, *Streckfus!*"

When Truman wandered back to his house, he told ol' Sook about his odd encounter with Nelle. She just shook her head. "Poor child. Her daddy works all the time and her mama's . . . well, she's a bit sick in the head."

"How do you mean?" he asked.

Sook glanced over at Nelle's house, running her hands through her thinning gray hair. She was small and slight but full of life—and opinions. "Her mama acts real peculiar sometimes—wanders the streets saying the strangest things to people. Some nights, she'll be playing her piano on the porch at *two in the morning,* waking up everyone in the neighborhood. Some say it's to block out the voices in her head."

"Can't she take some of your dropsy medicine for that?" asked Truman.

She shook her head. "Some things can't be cured—even by my special potion." Sook leaned in and whispered to him, "Sometimes her mama forgets to cook supper, and poor Mr. Lee and his children end up eating watermelon for dinner!"

No wonder Nelle acted strange.

That night, Truman went through his collection of books and picked out one just for her: a Rover Boys adventure called *The Mystery of the Wrecked Submarine.*

She'll like this one, he thought. He left it on top of the stone wall for her.

When he woke up the next morning, the book was gone.

2

The Prince
and the Pauper

It was a slow morning in the tiny town of Monroeville, Alabama, and that's saying something. A whole day had come and gone and Truman hadn't seen or heard from Nelle. He sat on the porch dutifully watching her house, with its gingerbread ornamentation and rusty wind vane. The oaks surrounding her home drooped with Spanish moss limp from the heat. Only a beat-up Hoover car being towed by a couple of old ponies seemed to offer any excitement.

The only folks outside in the sun were dark-skinned workers mowing lawns or sweeping sidewalks with their dogwood-brush brooms. Occasionally, blacksmith hammers would ring out in the alleyways and then go silent.

Truman got bored of waiting for her and wandered down the red-dirt roads that passed through the surrounding cotton fields and cattle pastures, then ambled along the creek, looking at the buzzards circling high overhead. After a spell of smelling fragrant chocolate vines and trying to convince the mockingbirds to copy his calls, he headed back home.

By the afternoon, he was sitting in the shade of his porch again, fanning himself in the numbing heat. He fell asleep to the scents of primrose and azalea that filled the yard. He awoke when the high-pitched scream of the sawmill whistle blew. He stretched out like a lazy cat, and it was only then that he noticed the two books he'd loaned Nelle sitting on the side table.

He shot upright, looking around for her, but

no one was in sight. When he picked the books up, he spotted a tiny pocket dictionary underneath them. On its red cover, it said: *The New Webster Dictionary and Complete Vest-Pocket Library—45,800 Words.* He cracked it open.

On the inside title page was handwritten: *To Nelle—The power of words can cause wars or create peace. Use yours wisely. —A.C.* Except *Nelle* was crossed out, and in childish pencil, someone had written *Bulldog* instead.

The next day, Truman was back on his wraparound porch being served sweet tea and cakes by Sook. He was dressed in a little suit and tie, and his wispy blond hair was pressed neatly against his forehead. She was in her usual blue gingham dress and white apron.

Sook had been his only companion since he'd arrived in Monroeville. Truth be told, everyone in Monroeville lived on farmer's hours—awake at sunrise, asleep by eight—except for Truman and Sook. While the other cousins all went to work during the week, the two odd ducks remained at home, sometimes with their part-time cook, a black woman named Little Bit.

Truman was treated by everyone like a delicate blue-blooded prince. No one could ever imagine him hitching a mule or chopping cotton under the hot sun, so, like they did with Sook, they just let him be.

His and Sook's job was to feed the chickens or pick the scuppernong grapes that grew along the fence made of animal bones that Cousin Jenny had built in the back. Sometimes they would walk the woods searching for herbs for Sook's special potions.

On Sundays, they'd pass the time making kites and decorating them with pictures from old magazines. In between, they'd laze about on the porch, where Sook would tell him stories or read the funnies out loud or generally just plain spoil him.

Sook was reading *Little Orphan Annie* to him when she looked up and smiled. "Why, hello, Miss Nelle. Come for tea?"

Nelle was covered head to toe in dirt and wearing torn overalls. Her eyes were stuck on Truman's neatly pressed outfit. "Ah don't think I'm dressed for it, Miss Sook," she said quietly.

"Oh, nonsense, Miss Nelle. No need to impress the likes of us. Miss Jenny tends to dress Tru up but he ain't fancy inside. He likes to eat hot biscuits with bacon drippings an' mayhaw jelly as much as the rest of us."

She heard Nelle's stomach grumbling. "I know you must like cake, dear. Would you care for some?" Sook held up the sweets for her to see.

Nelle's mouth practically watered. "Well . . . maybe. Just a bite, ma'am." She stepped up onto the porch and noticed her dirty feet. "I can just sit here on the steps, thank you, ma'am."

She sat and ate her cake while Sook continued to read the comics out loud. Truman watched Nelle devour the whole slice in three giant gulps. When she was done, she stood up as if she were about to leave. But then she just stayed put.

"How's your mama doing?" asked Sook, trying to make small talk.

Nelle furrowed her brow and stared at the ground. "She's away for a spell, down on the Gulf getting the treatment, Miss Sook. Daddy says she'll be good as new when they let her out."

"Out of where?" asked Truman.

Sook shot him a look that told him not to say anything more. "That's good, dear. Even I need a rest now and then, otherwise I'd go crazy too—"

Suddenly, Sook turned beet red. "Oh, look—we're all out of cake. I'll go get some more." She excused herself, whispering into Truman's ear, "Be nice."

Truman sat alone with Nelle, not sure what to say. He could feel the pocket dictionary she'd given him weighing down his coat. Maybe they could play a word game, since he'd been memorizing interesting words all morning. But then he had a better idea.

"Would you like another book to read?"

Her eyes lit up.

3
Island of Misfits

Truman took Nelle through the huge rambling house, which was decorated with all sorts of finery that his older cousin Jenny had collected over the years: ancient paper roses, delicate tchotchkes of all shapes and sizes, glass cases filled with fine china and silverware from all over the world.

They walked through the main room past two majestic pillars that rose to the high ceiling. In the dining room, they found Cousin Jenny herself, going through pages of her accounting ledgers. Even though she was past fifty, she was still pretty, with milky-white skin and reddish hair tied up in a bun.

Jenny's icy blue eyes observed them over her reading glasses. "Good morning, Miss Nelle. How's your mother doing?"

Truman interceded. "We're not supposed to talk about that, Cousin Jenny, on account of she's . . . you know, crazy," Truman whispered, a tad too loud.

Jenny frowned. "You'll have to forgive our Truman, dear. For such a smart little boy, he can sometimes be rather . . . rude."

"That's okay, Miss Jenny," said Nelle, admiring the surroundings. "Truman was just gonna loan me a new book, ma'am."

Jenny smiled. "That's fine, dear." It was then she noticed how dirty Nelle was. She sighed and turned back to her account books. "Well, you'll not be wanting to read *these* books, I can tell you that. But they do keep our finances in order so I can pay the bills to keep my hat store open and this house afloat."

Truman pulled Nelle into the hallway, which was lined from floor to ceiling with leather-bound volumes of all colors. Nelle was astounded. She had never seen so many.

"Not those, silly," said Truman. "Those are boring grown-up books. I have the real deal in my room."

"*Psst*, Tru."

It was old Cousin Bud, poking his head through his bedroom door. Bud had a headful of snow-white hair and yellow teeth from all the tobacco he smoked. "Fancy a card game, Little Chappie?"

"Not now, Cousin Bud, I have a guest."

Bud saw Nelle and nodded. "Mornin', Miss Nelle. How's your—"

Truman cut him off. "I'll stop by later and maybe we can play Go Fish, all right?"

Bud winked. "Sure thing, Little Chappie." He closed the door to his smoke-filled room.

Nelle scrunched her nose. "That tobacco smells funny."

"It's medicinal . . . for his asthma. Come on."

He guided her down the hall toward his room. But right when he was about to open his bedroom door, the door across from his swung open and there stood his cousin Callie. Callie was a teacher, wound tight, with coal-black hair and narrow gray eyes.

"And what do you think you're doing, young man?" she said, studying him. "Have you done your lessons?"

Truman crossed his arms and stood firm. "No, ma'am. Because it's *summer.* And you aren't my mother!"

"You impertinent little—I said you would be trouble as soon as you stepped foot in this house," she huffed. "If you had a mother who cared for you, then you wouldn't need *us* watching out for you! What you need is a good stick to your behind—"

Truman laughed. "You touch me, and Jenny will use that stick on you!"

Callie gasped; Nelle cleared her throat.

Callie hadn't noticed Nelle standing there. "Miss Nelle." She was not impressed with

Nelle's dirty appearance and didn't hesitate to say so. "I have students that have so much dirt in their ears, they could grow corn in them. But they work the farms. What's your excuse?"

"Don't pay her any mind, Nelle. She's just bored out of her gourd because she doesn't have any students to boss around during the summer," he said. "But if you must know, Cousin Callie, we are going into my room to look at books!"

Truman quickly dragged Nelle into his bedroom before Callie could say anything back. Arguing with her was a losing proposition.

He shut the door behind them. "Finally!" he said. "*This* is where I sleep."

Nelle looked around and was immediately drawn to a small shelf filled with children's books of all kinds. "Golly," she said, impressed. "Who needs a library when you got all these?"

She cocked her head sideways so she could read all the titles. "What book should I read next?" Nelle asked.

"Well, what do you fancy? Adventure?

Fantasy?" He assessed her mood. "Wait. I know just the thing . . ."

He went over to his bed, reached under the pillow, and pulled out a small green book. "I just finished this one. Sherlock Holmes, *The Adventure of the Creeping Man*," he said, handing it over.

Nelle gazed at the silhouette of the pipe-smoking Sherlock Holmes on the cover. "Is Watson in this one too?"

"Of course! They're a team. Everyone knows that when it comes to solving crime, two heads are better than one."

Nelle shrugged and tucked the book carefully into the front pocket of her overalls. It was then that she noticed there was another bed beside Truman's.

"This is really Sook's room," he said. "They just stuck me in here till I go back home again with my folks. I keep her company, poor old thing."

Nelle nodded. "I have to share a room with my older sisters, Bear and Weezie."

"You have a bear for a sister?" he asked.

"No, silly, that's just what we call her. She's fifteen years older than me and as big as a bear."

"I wish I had sisters to complain about," he said.

"No, you don't, you got it made—sleeping with your best friend and having books right by your bed. That's like . . . heaven."

She gazed dreamily at the bookshelf, running her finger along the titles: *Tom Swift in Captivity*, the Hardy Boys' *Secret of the Old Mill*, Nancy Drew's *The Hidden Staircase*.

"Sometimes I wish my sisters would disappear and leave me be." She sighed.

"You really think that?" he asked.

She grew quiet. "They're always joking around, saying how Mama found mc under a rock and that I don't really belong to the family on account of they're so much older than me. I asked Daddy about it and he said no such thing."

"You're lucky you have a daddy who's on your

side . . ." he said, though Nelle didn't really hear him.

She was glaring out the window at her house. "Last week, when three boys was making fun of me during a game of marbles, I just couldn't take it no more, so I had to make 'em cry."

"How'd you do that?" asked Truman.

"Rubbed their faces in the dirt. And do you know what my sisters did? They took the *boys'* side! Can you beat that?"

Truman knew what it was like not to feel wanted. "Is that your room over there? The window near the corner?"

She nodded.

"Well, I'll tell you what. If your sisters ever gang up on you again, just signal me and I'll sneak up to the window and scare the bejesus out them!" Truman giggled with delight.

Nelle snickered. There was something about this strange little boy she liked. "Thanks, Tru."

4

Too Hot for Mayhem

I think I'm gonna melt," whined Truman in that peculiar singsong voice of his. After an hour of playing pirates and knights of the Round Table, followed by two games of marbles and three of jacks, they'd run out of things to do.

Hot and tired, he and Nelle collapsed under the shade of the scuppernong grape arbor, where it was cool and breezy. They fanned themselves with the crossword-puzzle section of the *Monroe Journal,* which they'd also finished that morning.

"Reality is so boring! I wish something exciting would happen for once in this town. I've been here over a month and it's nothing like New Orleans."

"Well, it may not be all exciting like New Orleans," said Nelle. "But stuff still happens 'round here too. Why, just the other day, that black boy Edison was out in the town square drawing a crowd 'cause he could imitate anything you asked him to. He could do birds and horses, Mr. Barnett and his wooden leg, the cotton-gin machine, anything. I asked him to do the mail-carrier train, and he started shuffling his feet in the dirt, chugging and tooting like a train whistle! *That's* not something you see every day."

Truman was unimpressed. "I suppose we could go down to the drugstore and get some free candy again." He rolled his eyes up into his head and began twitching and shaking as if he were having a fit.

"Stop it. You just about gave Mr. Yarborough a heart attack. His son's an epileptic, you know? And I think he knows candy doesn't stop a fit."

Truman shrugged. "He still gave us free licorice."

"Yeah, to get rid of us."

Truman sat up. "What we need is some big-city excitement. Like . . . just imagine if somebody disappeared. Or there was a murder in town! Then we'd *really* have something to do."

Nelle stared at him like he was nuts. "Just what the heck would *we* do with a murder or a kidnapping?"

"Why, solve it, of course. We could be detectives." He snapped his fingers. "I could be Sherlock and you could be Watson! The brains and the muscle. See?" He pretended to be smoking a pipe.

"Why cain't I be—oh, never mind. No one ever gets murdered here anyways. Why, when General Lee himself came to Monroeville, he called it the most boring place on earth!"

They both stared into the deep blue Alabama

sky and counted bits of floating white cotton fluff that escaped from the cotton gin across town.

"Well, he got that right," said Truman eventually. "I guess it is too hot for mayhem. The only place where anything is happening is probably down at the swimming hole at Hatter's Mill. We could go swimming and at least cool off. It's no Lake Pontchartrain, but it'll do."

Nelle made a face. "You don't want to go down there."

Truman's eyes lit up. "Why not? Are there gators? Is it *dangerous?*"

Nelle wiped the sweat off her brow. She knew the boys who hung out at Hatter's Mill. Billy Eugene and his pals would beat the snot out of a boy like Truman. The least she could do was keep him out of trouble.

"No, it's just not . . ." She couldn't think of a good excuse.

"What?" He tilted his head, curious. "You're not chicken, are you? Can't you swim?"

Nelle was offended. "No, I ain't chicken, and

yes, I can swim rings around you!" She stared him down good. He just smiled back at her.

"Fine, let's go, then," she said. "But on one condition."

"What's that?" he asked innocently.

"You have to dress more . . . normal."

"Normal?" said Truman. He blew the long wispy strands of hair out of his eyes. "Since when is *normal* any fun? I mean, look at you. You're a girl and you dress like a boy!"

Nelle tugged on her overalls. She knew it was useless to argue. Truman was only a year older than her, but he acted like he was already grown up. "Fine," she said. "But don't blame me if some boys throw you off the roof of the old millhouse. You're always starting something."

Truman grinned like an impish pixie looking for trouble. "Who, *me?* I can't help it if I'm a . . . *harbinger.*" He waited for a reaction from Nelle, who plain refused to play his little word games. He whipped out his miniature dictionary anyway and opened it to a marked page. "It means 'innovating pioneer'—"

"Ah don't care what it means, *Streckfus*," she said, pretending to ignore him.

Truman jutted out his lower jaw and scowled. He hated when she called him that. "Suit yourself, Na-il Har-puh!"

She stuck her tongue out; he just shrugged.

"Well, go on, then, get dressed," she said. "I'll meet you over there, you ol' . . . *bellwether*."

Truman giggled. Nelle was the only person he'd met who was as good as him with words.

Of course, everyone was at the pond at Hatter's Mill that afternoon. Billy Eugene, Hutch, Doofie, and Twiggs Butts were horsing around, diving into the water and shouting things at the other kids. The girly girls, who were afraid to get their hair wet, made cute comments back at them, trying to get them to dive off the roof of the mill. Nelle kept to herself, wading through the cool waters by the shore, letting the fish tickle her legs.

Suddenly, everything went quiet. Nelle looked up and saw Edison, that gangly boy whose skin was so dark, she thought he might be a real African. He was standing at the edge of the pond in shorts that were made from an old sack of flour, dipping his toe in the water and imitating a gurgling stream.

"Just what do you think you're doing, boy?" Billy Eugene shouted.

Edison looked around and saw everyone staring at him. "Just dippin' my toe and talking to the stream," he said quietly.

The boys laughed. "You know no coloreds is allowed here. You got to go over to the Negro pond."

Edison looked confused. "The Negro pond is closed ever since y'all dammed it up." He pointed down a ways to the drained part of the pond, which was only a bowl of dried-up mud now.

"What's a little mud, boy?" said Billy. "It ain't like you gonna get any darker!" He and his friends had a good laugh at that.

Nelle could see Edison's jaw clenching. She hated when bullies picked on kids who couldn't fight back, and a colored boy hitting a white boy? That was not allowed. She wanted to go over there herself and punch Billy Eugene in the nose, just so he'd mind his own business. Then she heard someone singing.

"I found a million-dollar baby . . . in a five-an'-ten-cent store!" The singing was followed by whistling and then Truman appeared from around the bend. With all the subtlety of a peacock, he strutted down the path with an umbrella, acting like Little Lord Fauntleroy.

"Heya, Edison!" He waved, pausing for all to admire his swimwear.

While all the boys were barefoot and wearing hand-me-down swim trunks made of old cut-off pants, Truman had shown up in a bright red Hawaiian shirt, white pool sandals, and baby-blue designer swim trunks that his mother had sent him from a trip she'd taken to Florida.

Nelle thought she was going to die of embarrassment. When Edison tried to touch Truman's shirt, Tru playfully swatted his hand away. "Don't *touch!* Just admire with your eyes like everyone else." He winked at Edison, then whispered, "Now follow me."

Edison smiled and followed along.

Truman was undersize for his age, but he held that big head of his high and proceeded toward Nelle with as much style as a fancy prince from Monaco — much to everyone's wide-eyed amazement. Nelle was sure the boys would drag him into the mud with Edison, but nobody said a thing — their jaws were stuck on the ground.

"Why be normal when you can have fun?" he said as he and Edison waded up to Nelle. "That's how we do it in *New Or-leeeens.*"

They made for quite a picture — the little prince, the tomboy, and the gangly black kid who imitated things. For now, it would pass for excitement in Monroeville.

Only Truman could turn a sleepy Saturday upside down.

5

Bamboozled

O kay, open your eyes," said Nelle.

Truman pulled Nelle's hands away from his face. He found himself smack in the center of the town square facing the Monroeville courthouse, the oldest and most stately building in the county, even if the clock in its impressive tower always ran five minutes slow.

"What are we doing here?" he asked. He'd wanted to go swimming again but Nelle had had other plans.

"You said you wanted some excitement. Well, here it is," she said as if it were obvious.

"The courthouse?"

She poked him in the shoulder. "Dummy. Where do you think all the criminals end up? I thought you liked Sherlock Holmes?"

Truman's eyes grew wide. "Do you think they'll try a *murder* case?"

"Who knows? I come here all the time an' there's always some kinda mischief going on. Why, sometimes it's better than going to the picture show."

Truman pondered this. "Wait. How come they let *you* in? Isn't this place for grownups?"

"Heck, no!" she said, pulling him along. "They know me 'cause I got connections . . ."

She headed up to the main entrance, where a few town policemen were milling about. One officer, a lumbering oaf with a large shaggy beard, spotted her straightaway. "Morning, Miss Nelle. Looking for your daddy?"

"Naw, we're here to watch the new case."

The policeman raised his eyebrows and

chuckled. "Well, this one's a doozy, Miss Nelle. I hope you and your friend here don't scare easy."

Truman didn't care to be put in his place. "*We* don't scare easy. Why, I've seen danger up close, sir. I'll have you know that when I was living in New Orleans, our neighbor kept a tiger in his basement."

"You don't say," said the cop.

"I do, Officer. And boy, that tiger was something fierce! He'd already eaten *two* people alive that I knew about."

"Why didn't he eat you, then?" asked Nelle.

"Well . . . I guess tigers like me," Truman answered, matter of fact. "Whenever I petted him, he purred just like a kitty. One day, the mailman came by and would've been swallowed whole if I hadn't been there!"

"Huh, don't that beat all," said the cop, not buying a word of it. "Well, I guess it's true what they say—tigers don't eat shrimp!" He cackled.

The officers had a good laugh, then headed

inside the courthouse. Truman stayed put, stewing on the front steps.

"Well, ain't you coming? You don't want to miss the show," said Nelle.

Truman didn't budge, so Nelle grabbed him by the hand and led him inside, squeezing between the adults in the lobby to reach a small stairway at the far end of the room. "Come on. Best seats in the house," she said, heading up the wooden steps. They came to a door that said FOR COLORED ONLY, but Nelle ignored the sign and pushed on past it.

They came out onto an empty balcony that overlooked the airy courtroom. Down below, there was an assortment of characters: the oafish policeman from outside, a crotchety old judge in a black gown, a weary-looking court stenographer, and an enormously fat lawyer conferring quietly with his client, a white woman dressed, oddly, like a princess from India, in gold and black robes. Across from them, sitting calmly behind a table, was a man wearing a plain, dark three-piece suit and horn-rimmed glasses, carefully studying everyone in the room.

"Your daddy works here?" asked Truman as they sat down. "He's not that awful policeman, is he?"

"Course not." Nelle pointed at the man in the glasses. "That's him. That's A.C."

Nelle's daddy checked his pocket watch. He seemed like a serious, thoughtful man.

"A.C.? What kind of name is that?" asked Truman.

"A.C. stands for Amasa Coleman, but people just call him A.C. ever since I can remember. He's a lawyer and a deacon . . . *and* the editor of the *Monroe Journal*."

Truman felt a pang of jealousy pass through him.

"*Psst!*" Nelle tried to get her daddy's attention. "A.C.!"

A.C. ignored her. He checked his watch again and considered the empty chair beside him.

"You don't call him Daddy?"

"Naw. Everyone calls him A.C., why shouldn't I?" she said. "Hey, look, something's going on."

A.C. approached the judge, who then called the other lawyer up to the bench as well. They spoke in hushed tones, back and forth, occasionally looking at the empty chair.

The judge banged his gavel. "Is Mr. Archulus Persons in attendance?" he asked gruffly. "Bailiff?"

The policeman spoke up. "No, Your Honor. Mr. Persons has not yet been seen today."

The judge nodded, making a note. "Very well. A warrant shall be issued for his arrest this afternoon . . . Is the next case ready?"

Nelle looked disappointed. "Holy cow. Looks like the suspect fled! Hey, that should be exciting—"

"We should go," Truman said softly. He acted as if he'd seen a ghost.

"Oh, come on, another case is coming up.

One's as good as the next. Why, last week, Mr. Cooper was accused of stealing Miss Anna Mae's peach cobbler from her window—"

Truman suddenly jumped up and headed for the stairs.

"Truman! Where you going?"

He disappeared down the steps, but she was right on his tail. "Tru! Wait!"

He ran through the lobby, down the courthouse steps, and right onto Alabama Avenue. When she finally grabbed him by the elbow in the middle of the street, she was so winded and confused, she didn't even see the automobile barreling down on them.

6

A Close Call

The blaring horn and skidding tires chilled them to the bone — they found themselves suddenly staring straight into a pair of headlights.

"Truman! There you are!"

Truman blinked and saw a shadowy figure standing up in the convertible, peering at him through the flurry of red dust that had been kicked up by the tires.

"Daddy?" he said, in shock.

Nelle let go of his arm. She'd wet her pants.

While she stood there red-faced and unsure what to do next, Truman walked around to the passenger side, and there was his father, sporting a straw Panama hat and grinning ear to ear.

"Daddy," he said breathlessly.

"Come on, son," he said, opening the passenger door for him. "We got to go. *Now.*"

Truman climbed into the car and dove into his father's arms.

His dad squeezed him tight as he glanced around nervously. "I wanted to surprise you. Are you surprised?"

Truman nodded, unable to believe his eyes. He hadn't seen his father in two months.

"I'll say he's surprised!" said Nelle, turning her embarrassment into ire. "Just where have you *been?* Why, if my daddy ever left me alone for so long, I'd just—"

"Who's your charming friend, Truman?" he asked. "He's quite a feisty kid."

Nelle's face turned even brighter red. "I'm a *she,* darn it! Just 'cause I don't wear a dress don't mean I ain't fit ta wear one!"

Truman's daddy tipped his hat. "Well, you must be queen of the tomboys, aren't ya, darling?" He nudged Truman. "Never mess with a feisty woman, Tru. I learned that from your mother. Now, we really got to go—"

Truman jumped up, excited. "Is Mother here too?"

His father started up the car, grinding it into gear. "More or less . . ."

Truman looked up at him with puppy-dog eyes. "Does that mean we're all going home together?"

The color drained from his father's face. "We've got family business to discuss, Truman. Let's go back to the house."

The man tipped his hat to Nelle once again. "Nice to have met you, little fella. Name's Archulus Persons."

Nelle blinked. "Wait a sec . . . Archulus?"

He gunned the engine and left Nelle standing in the road.

"Glad to see you're making friends," Arch said as he quickly steered off the main road and headed up an empty alleyway. He seemed nervous.

"Are you taking me home?" asked Truman.

Arch hemmed and hawed. "Truman . . . I know it's been hard on you, son. If your mother wasn't so stubborn, we'd all be back together again. But she has all these ideas of moving to an expensive big city like New York . . . she thinks we're millionaires!" He moaned. "Oh, I just don't know what to do."

They drove in silence. Truman had so many questions. But this one popped out: "How come you were wanted in court?"

Arch raised his eyebrows. "What are you talking about, son? Why would they want ol' Archulus in a court of law?"

"That's what I thought. But when the judge called your name in the courtroom—"

Arch's face turned beet red. "Oooh . . . *that*. That was nothing. Simply a disagreement that happened over in Burnt Corn—or was it Cobb Creek? Was there a woman there who was dressed like she was from India?"

Truman thought about it and remembered such a woman. "With gold and black robes?"

"That's the one. She was the Great Hadjah's widow, unfortunately," he said, nervously looking over his shoulder. "God rest his soul."

"Who's he?" asked Truman.

Arch acted incredulous. "You mean you've never heard of the Great—" He slapped his forehead. "No, of course not. He passed before we had a chance to perform here in town."

Truman's eyes lit up. "You ran a show?"

Arch grinned. "*Show* is selling it short. *Extravaganza* is more like it. 'Buried Alive!'" he proclaimed, just like P. T. Barnum himself. "The greatest miracle of modern times!"

"You buried him *alive?*"

"You should've seen it, Tru. See, I found this Egyptian fella over in Mississippi. Could hold his breath for long periods. He'd slow his heart rate down until he went into a state of hibernation for hours!"

"Really?" said Truman, amazed.

"Well, for one hour, at least. He'd show up dressed like an Indian prince and we'd bury him for an hour in a coffin right in the town square! People ate it up, betting he couldn't last the whole sixty minutes, but he always did. Made a fortune!"

"So what happened to him?"

Arch wiped his brow. "Well, the last show, we drew *such* a huge crowd that by the time I took everyone's money and wrote down their bets, almost two hours had passed . . . and so, sadly, had the Great Hadjah."

"You mean . . . he *died*?"

Arch nodded glumly. "Turned out an hour was about as long as he could go. Who knew? Poor fella. Unfortunately, I lost everything too. And now this woman is trying to sue me for her husband's share. Ridiculous! He was the one always bragging about how long he could

last underground. But who's always left holding the bag in the end? Old Arch, that's who."

He pulled up by the animal-bone fence behind Cousin Jenny's house and shut the engine
off; the car rattled to a stop. He sat there a moment looking at the house. "Now, Truman,
not a word of this to your mother. She's mad
enough at me as it is. I don't need her knowing
we might lose even more. But I'll make it up to
her. I've another scheme in mind. There's this
boxer—"

But Truman was already out and running
toward the house. He had this overwhelm-
ing feeling that if his mother just saw his face,
she'd realize how much she missed him, and
the family might come together once again.

7
Running the Gauntlet

When Truman's daddy drove off, leaving Nelle alone in the middle of the street, she didn't know quite what to do. It wasn't until she saw Twiggs Butts standing in front of Dr. Fripp's general store that she knew something was wrong. He seemed puzzled—that is, until he started giggling at her.

"What's so funny, Butts?" said Nelle, getting ready to wipe that grin off his face.

He pointed at the front of her pants. Her eyes wandered down till she saw the spot where she had wet herself. Unfortunately, red dust was now sticking to the wetness.

She gasped and turned an even darker shade of red. She tried wiping the dirt away, but that only made it look worse. She wanted to hit Butts, but that would have to come later.

Instead, she ran.

She wasn't thinking straight and just barreled right down the middle of the road, trying to keep her hands in front of her. Everyone seemed to be staring at her. The more people she recognized, the faster she ran.

Luckily, she lived only two blocks from the town square. When she came to her street, she ran straight past Bud, who was smoking his pipe at the edge of his yard. "Top of the day, Miss Nelle—"

It was a good thing the front door to her house was open, otherwise she might have plowed right through it. She ran straight into her room. There, to her horror, her two older sisters, Weezie and Bear, were sitting on the beds chatting away.

She froze right in front of them, and of course their eyes went straight to her embarrassment. They both burst out laughing.

"Honestly, Nelle, if you're gonna wet the bed, you should probably *be* in bed when you do it."

"It was an accident!" she shouted. Her eyes quickly scanned the room for new clothes before they could make another joke. Unfortunately, the only clean garment sitting out was the dress her mother had made for her that she had never worn.

The sisters started laughing even harder when they realized her predicament. She clenched her jaw and grabbed the dress. It was better than spending another second wearing what she had on.

"Goodness! Nelle wearing a dress? What is this world coming to?" cracked Bear.

When Nelle ran into the hall closet and

slammed the door, they laughed even harder. She was so embarrassed and angry at herself. Maybe she would just stay in there forever and see how they liked that!

She took off her overalls and threw them to the floor. She stared at the dress in her hands. She hadn't worn one since . . . her mother's birthday, two years ago. She remembered hating that dress so much that afterward, she deliberately ripped it so badly that it couldn't be repaired.

She sat down on an old suitcase next to her dad's golf clubs and covered her head with the dress. She wasn't gonna cry. Instead, she took a deep breath . . . and suddenly, she could smell her mother's scent on the outfit. That made her remember some other things about her mother's birthday. Like how she had tried to help her with a crossword puzzle that morning. Or how her abundantly plump mother had danced gracefully around the living room as the sunlight poured in through the bay window. And how they tended to her favorite flower boxes on the front porch together and picked some winter lilac and lavender-edged roses for her party. But most of all, she remembered how beautifully her mother had played the piano and how, in the middle of the party, in front of all the guests, Nelle sang "Tea for Two" while her mother played along.

It was the only time they'd ever performed a song together.

8

The Cold Hard Truth

The back door to Jenny's house was wide open. Truman ran in and stopped in his tracks. The kitchen was empty. He listened, but all he could hear was the sound of his heart racing. Then he heard voices. They were coming from the front sitting room.

He walked slowly toward them. The house was quiet, the bedroom doors all closed. Women were talking in hushed tones.

One of them was Sook. The other was his mother.

Just the sound of her voice made Truman smile. He thought maybe he'd sneak up behind her, wrap his hands over her eyes—and then she'd shriek with delight and hug the daylights out of him.

Then he heard what they were saying.

"He's missed you so, Lillie Mae," whispered Sook. "Sometimes I find him crying in bed and I just hold him for a good hour till he falls asleep. He needs his mama. He needs you."

"Oh, I don't know, Sook," said his mother. "I don't wish to sound mean but . . . but I just can't stand the sight of my son—it's like he's not even mine."

There was silence for a moment.

"That's a horrible thing to say—and it's nonsense, Lillie Mae! I saw you birth him myself!" said Sook.

"That's not what I mean. I know it's loathsome of me, but that boy is so outlandish. He does not act like a normal boy should. He's just like his con man of a father—living in a fantasy world and dragging me into it."

"You can't be serious, Lillie Mae. He's just a child."

"The idea of settling down with him and Archie makes me feel like a trapped animal—it'll never work!" There was a pause and then she added, "Because of that, I've decided: Truman's going to live here from now on."

"Oh, Lillie Mae, Jenny won't stand for it. I don't think you know what this will do to the boy. It'll send him over the edge."

"Well, I never asked for a child! Look what he's done to my figure. I'm only twenty-six but I feel ragged beyond my years. Time is wasting away and the last thing I need is to be stuck at home with that precocious little—"

She looked up and saw Truman standing in the doorway of the kitchen. He was fighting back the tears.

She sighed, putting on a fake smile with her

ruby-red lipstick. "Truman. You'll be happier here, darling. Trust me. I'm just no good as a mother."

He didn't want to hear it. He ran back through the house, down the steps, and straight into the arms of his father.

"Whoa, whoa, little fella. What's wrong?" He felt Truman's tears on his neck. When Arch looked up and saw Lillie Mae standing by the door, he grew angry. "Really? You couldn't wait for me to come inside before you told him?"

She shrugged and lit a cigarette. "He overheard me. What can I say?"

Arch picked Truman up and walked him to the side of the house. "Hey, buddy, I'm sorry. You shouldn't have heard that."

"I don't understand," said Truman, his eyes shut tight.

Arch sighed. "All I can say is, every cloud has a silver lining, so . . . I'm gonna give you yours now."

Truman opened one eye. "You're not going to leave me?"

Arch grimaced and knelt down so Truman could stand. "Look, son. I know we said this would be temporary, like a summer vacation. But the truth is . . . me and your mom . . . both want different things out of life . . ."

"And what about me?" whimpered Truman. "Don't you want me?"

Arch couldn't look him in the eye. "I will do what I can to come back and get you. I just need time. I have some new ideas that I think will make us a fortune, but I can't have you tagging along."

"But we worked on the steamboats together . . ."

"That was then. Now . . . you belong in school, where you can grow up and become smarter than your old man. I know it's not what you want to hear . . . but I hope this will help make you a little happier for now."

He spun Truman around to face a rather large object covered with a tarp.

"I know how much you followed Lindbergh and his flight across the Atlantic. I figure that by the time you grow up, the world will be looking for another Lucky Lindy and maybe you can be just as famous . . ."

Arch slowly pulled off the tarp and revealed a miniature bright green Ford Tri-Motor airplane with a red propeller. It was big enough for Truman to sit in—kind of an oversize tricycle with wings. The way the sun gleamed off the propeller made it look as beautiful as anything Truman had ever seen.

"Is that the one from the store?" asked Truman.

Arch reached into his pocket and pulled out an aviator's cap and goggles. "Sure is, the very same one you wanted when you was a pup. That's from me to you. You'll be the envy of every kid in the neighborhood. And as soon as I make my mark and get enough money to settle down again, I'll come back for you."

"Do you promise?" asked Truman.

"Of course, buddy."

"You promised me a dog last time."

Arch nodded. "Now, that was your cousin Jenny's fault. 'No dogs in my house!'" he said, imitating her. "But she didn't say no airplanes. So why don't you go try it out before it takes off without you? That's the top of the line!"

He put the cap and goggles on Truman's head. "And you're way better-looking than that Lindy fella too!"

Truman climbed into his plane and felt the controls. It looked like what he imagined a real plane looked like. It felt good. He gave the thumbs-up to his daddy and pulled the goggles down over his eyes. "Contact!" he said.

Arch made a big show of spinning the propeller, and off Truman went, cycling the plane into the street as if it really could fly. He imagined building up enough speed until the wheels actually left the ground and he was suddenly airborne, flying out into the wild blue yonder.

There's Cousin Bud in his cotton patch! And there's Hatter's Mill with Edison jumping into the deep end. And there's Billy Eugene, that scoundrel.

Truman would dive-bomb him and his friends and chase them off the path.

Truman was having so much fun in his imagination, he didn't even notice Arch and Lillie Mae driving away.

9

A Secret Plan

Truman was moody for the longest time after that. Nelle couldn't even get him to come out to play. She begged her to let her ride his Tri-Motor plane but he flat-out refused. He wasn't being mean; he just didn't feel like seeing anyone. Instead, he stayed in his room for weeks on end.

Sook couldn't stand to see Truman carrying on and tried everything to snap him out of his spell. In the beginning, she sat by his bed and hand-fed him like he was a small sparrow that had fallen from its nest. Later, in moments of quiet, Sook told him about the grass harp that she'd heard as a child—the sounds the wind made when it wafted through the rolling fields of the tall grasses nearby. She would then gently whisper in his ear until he fell asleep.

Cousin Jenny also grew concerned. "As long as I'm alive and running this house, you'll have a roof over your head, young man. You'll not lack for clothing on your back or food in your belly. Your mama doesn't deserve your love."

His cousin Bud would take him to his cotton patch on the other side of the hill, just to get him out once in a while. Usually, they did this in silence, Truman riding glumly on Bud's shoulders with Bud's whiskers tickling Truman's legs. But this time, Bud spoke.

"Life is a heck of a hill to climb, Little Chappie. But if it gets too steep for ya, just get down on your hands and knees and keep going. Sooner or later, you'll get over the hump," he said, wheezing.

They made it up and over the hill.

At the cotton patch, Truman would hang out quietly in front of the shack of Bud's only worker, Black John White (so called to avoid confusion with White John Black, the tobacconist). While Bud and Black John surveyed the crop, John's wife would make hot biscuits with bacon drippings for Truman, but it did little to cheer him up.

One day, as the sunlight was fading and dusk turned the grass around their home from green to orange, Truman asked, "Bud, how come I don't have a real home like other kids?"

Bud, who was normally calm, put his hands on Truman's shoulders and looked him square in the eye. "Tru, *this* is your home. You are my blood kin, my second cousin thrice removed. But blood kin's not the most important kin. Do you know what is?"

"No, sir."

"Love kin. And that comes from the heart. That's why this is your home. Now, you got every reason to mope. Can't blame you for that. But if you just look around, you'll see—you're already home, Little Chappie."

Nelle felt lonely without her friend. To cheer her up, A.C. took her golfing at the local course, which she liked because it made her feel like an adult. She caddied and occasionally took a swing under A.C.'s supervision. Her father always wore his dark three-piece suit, even on the golf course, which made for quite a sight with his herky-jerky swing. But between holes, they'd talk.

"I don't understand how come Tru won't play with me no more, A.C. I never seen him in such a state," she said.

"Well, just be patient and he'll come around. The situation with his father can't be helping."

Nelle had been dying to ask. "Did you ever arrest him?"

A.C. chose his words carefully. "No. Judge decided he didn't want to waste time chasing him down. He believes Arch'll mess up soon enough, and when he does, the court will still be there."

"Poor Truman," said Nelle. "It must be awful having a daddy who's a liar."

A.C. put his hand on her shoulder. "Judge not, lest ye be judged, daughter."

"What's that supposed to mean?"

"It means don't be so quick to cast judgment; wait until you know the whole truth. Truman's father may not be trustworthy, but I believe he's trying to provide in the only way he knows how."

"That don't make it any easier on Tru," she mumbled.

He stopped and considered the next hole. "No, it doesn't. But what you can do is just be kind to Truman. He needs someone in his corner. Sometimes, a small gesture of friendship can make all the difference."

Soon enough, Nelle came up with a plan to cheer up her friend. But she needed a wingman for her project, and she looked to one of

Truman's youngest cousins, Big Boy, to help her bring Truman back to life.

Big Boy was the son of Lillie Mae's sister, Mary Ida. His real name was Jennings, which was why everyone preferred his nickname. He and Truman were the same age and he lived on a farm just outside Monroeville. He was not a particularly big boy, though, except at birth, when he weighed over twelve pounds. His growth slowed as he got older, and by seven, he was just an average-size kid. He wore Coke-bottle glasses, which made his eyes look as big as an owl's. As he heard Nelle's plan, his big eyes grew even wider.

"So . . . it's gonna be like a secret hideaway?" he asked.

"More 'n that, Big Boy. It's gonna be our headquarters," she said proudly.

"Headquarters for what?" he asked.

"Why, for our detective agency, that's what. The only thing that's gonna shake Truman out of his stink is a good ol' mystery that needs solving."

"But there ain't no mystery in Monroeville," said Big Boy. "'Cept why the courthouse clock is always five minutes slow."

"Well, I was reading about Sherlock," said Nelle. "And he said, 'To a great mind, nothing is little.'"

"I don't get it," said Big Boy.

Nelle tried to spell it out for him. "Silly, just 'cause you don't see something in front of your eyes don't mean it ain't happening. Once we start looking, who knows what we're gonna dig up around here?"

Big Boy still appeared puzzled.

"Look." She pointed to the sketch of the hideout she had drawn in crayon on the back of a piece of wrapping paper. "Sherlock and Watson had 221B Baker Street. This'll be our headquarters."

Big Boy raised his glasses to take a closer look. "A treehouse?"

The drawing was crude, but he got the idea. The treehouse was held aloft by a double chinaberry tree, one trunk on each side of the stone wall that ran between their properties. It looked like a couple of trees dancing with a house floating in their arms. A rope ladder went up the trunk of one to a trapdoor you could lock from inside in case of intruders. It had all kinds of nifty features: a porthole with a telescope for spying and a can-on-a-string telephone that connected to both Truman's and Nelle's rooms, in case an emergency arose.

"Wow," he said. "Can we put in a fire pole? You know, for quick escapes."

"Excellent idea, Big Boy," said Nelle. "Once Tru sees this, he'll be back to his old self in no time."

Of course, Cousin Bud and Black John White ended up building most of it for them. Nelle and Big Boy hauled leftover wood from the old, abandoned icehouse at the edge of the field, handed hammers and nails when needed, and put all the finishing touches on it themselves. In two weeks, Nelle's plan was realized.

Truman knew Nelle was up to something but he couldn't quite see what because the corner of the house blocked his view. But something was afoot. Every time he ventured out to have a look-see, Sook or Bud would suddenly need his help or challenge him to a game of Go Fish.

He would find out soon enough.

10
Headquarters
in the Sky

One morning, Truman awoke to what he thought was the sound of fighting outside. He poked his head out the window and spotted Nelle walking along the top of the stone wall that separated their houses. She was doing battle with some unseen foe, wearing a patch over one eye and a pirate hat made of newspaper. Truman was so amused, he yelled, "Watch out for the gators!"

Nelle lifted her eye patch and smiled at him. "Ahoy!"

Truman pointed again at the invisible gator; she took a stone from her pocket and pegged a log next to the wall. "Got him! I ain't afraid of no gators! Look what I can do!" She attempted a somersault but took a tumble and fell off her side of the wall.

"Nelle?" Truman cried, worried.

Nelle popped up, pretending to fight off a fallen branch. "Snakes! Help me, Tru!"

Truman ran down in his pajamas and slippers. He poked his head out on the front porch, but all was quiet. "Nelle?" he called out. He crept up to the wall and peered over. She was nowhere to be found.

"Psst!" Truman heard a voice from far overhead. He followed the sound up the huge double chinaberry tree and suddenly he saw it: the magnificent secret headquarters Nelle and Big Boy had built.

It was one of the greatest things he'd ever seen.

Truman spotted a pair of feet sticking out the flap that covered the entrance. Even though he was still in his PJs, he decided to climb up the ladder. When he reached the top, he couldn't believe his eyes. Every detail was perfect. A section for playing marbles and jacks. A lookout for spying. A board for drawing clues and whatnot. Jars for collecting bugs, rocks, and other scientific discoveries, and an open skylight for stargazing. Even a fire pole for quick escapes. Best of all was the sign gracing the front of the treehouse: NO GROWNUPS ALLOWED!

He crawled in and found Nelle lying down on a mattress stuffed with hay, reading. He was speechless.

"What happened to the snakes?" he finally asked.

"Oh, Ah kilt them all," she said, like it was no big deal. "I hate snakes."

He noticed she was reading one of the Rover Boys mysteries and plopped down next to her. She closed the book on him.

"Read your own," she said. Nelle reached under her pillow and produced a purple volume. "A.C. brung back it back from his trip to Selma."

New books were hard to come by in Monroeville, though occasionally traveling gypsies brought some from their distant wanderings. So whenever a new title appeared, it was like finding a dollar coin in the street—it was a treat.

Truman glanced at the cover and saw the familiar profile with a pipe and deerstalker cap. "Sherlock Holmes!" He breathed in with delight.

"Not only that—look!" She reached for a box on the shelf and handed it to him.

"What's this?" he asked.

"Just a little something me and Big Boy whipped up."

"A gift?" He tore into it, excited.

"More like . . . something you'll be needin', Tru." She watched as he pulled out a green baseball cap with another bill sewn onto the back.

"A deerstalker cap. Just like Sherlock," Nelle said proudly.

Truman stared at it for the longest time. It was too wonderful for words.

"Put it on," she said.

He carefully placed it on his head. "How's it look?"

"Just like the real thing," she said. "You know what this means, right?"

Truman pretended to smoke a pipe. "What?"

"The game's afoot!" she exclaimed.

Truman nodded. "We just need to find our own mystery is all."

She picked up a magnifying glass from the shelf and started examining a dead bug. "I have a feeling a mystery will reveal itself soon," she said. "All we have to do is wait."

11

The Hound of Monroeville

That night, it rained so hard it felt like the town was trapped under a waterfall. Gales of wind and water and who knew what else came pouring out of the sky. Truman had never seen such a deluge, but Cousin Jenny wouldn't let him stand out on the porch to watch. "You'll catch your death from it!" she said.

So he sat in his room in the dark, watching the rain come down. Lightning lit up the yard from time to time, followed by a low rumbling that grew louder and louder till it shook the glass windows around him.

It was in between lightning strikes that Truman heard a strange whimpering sound. "Do you hear that, Sook?"

Sook was trying to sleep. "Thought that was you being scared of the lightning."

He heard it again. It was coming from outside. "No, that sounds like somebody's crying."

Sook came over to the window and they both pressed their faces against the glass. A huge crack of lightning cut across the sky—and that's when they saw it: a black and white puppy, wet and shivering, in the backyard.

"Oh my!" she cried out.

"It's a dog. It looks lost," he said. "I'm going outside."

"But, Tru—"

Truman grabbed a towel and headed through the kitchen, tiptoeing so that Jenny wouldn't hear him. He peeked out the back door and over the edge of the porch. The wind was howling and he couldn't see a thing through the downpour. When the sky lit up again, he spotted the puppy sitting in the mud off the back steps.

Truman was barefoot, but he threw the towel over his head and ran quickly out to the dog. He hated getting wet, especially in his pajamas. He wasn't sure if the dog would bite but it seemed so helpless, shivering, with those big brown eyes staring up at him. Truman looked around but there was no one else in sight.

The bedroom window cracked open and Sook peered out into the rain. "Well, don't just stand there, Truman. Bring it in."

Truman gazed down at the puppy. The dog was sopping wet and looked like it hadn't eaten in a while. It had been a long time since Truman had felt sorry for anyone other than himself. He quickly took the towel off and wrapped it around the dog. "I'm gonna call you Queenie," he said.

Queenie wagged its tail.

He struggled to pick up the dog and managed to kind of drag it up onto the porch, where Sook was waiting with another towel and a piece of chicken.

He put the dog down and dried it off as it wolfed down the snack. "She's hungry," he said. The dog started licking Truman's face. "Stop it now, Queenie." He giggled.

"He likes you," said Sook.

Truman kissed the dog on the nose. "She. Her name is Queenie."

Sook bent down and peeked under the towel. "He. And you can't name a he Queenie. Call him Rover or some boy's name."

Truman didn't care. He'd always wanted a dog. Arch had promised him one long ago and he'd picked out the name Queenie because it came to him in a dream about Queen Mary.

"The dog's name is Queenie and that's all there is to it." He hugged the dog and the dog licked his ear. "Oh, Queenie, I'm so glad you showed up."

"Looks like some kind of rat terrier," said Sook.

Truman petted his spotted fur. Sook put another piece of chicken down on the porch and Queenie sniffed around for it, then gobbled it right up.

"Just as I thought, a bloodhound," said Truman. "Perfect for Sherlock's next case."

The light in Jenny's room clicked on and Truman could see her shadow approaching the window. "Quick, Sook, let's get him inside, before Jenny finds out."

They picked Queenie up in the towel and brought the dog inside. Queenie started to whimper until Truman leaned into his ear and whispered, "Shhh, everything will be aaallll right."

Once they were secure in their bedroom and Sook brought in some food and a bowl of water, Queenie settled in just fine. Truman made the dog a little bed next to the Tri-Motor plane he kept in the corner. Queenie was tuckered out, so he just plopped down and started snoring.

"We can keep Queenie, right, Sook?" he asked.

Truman could tell Sook was taken by the dog. "Well, we can keep it in here till Jenny finds out. Then you'll have to deal with him . . . I mean her—*it*."

"Don't worry. Jenny would never throw out a homeless dog," said Truman. "Least not one as cute as Queenie."

It took only a few days for Jenny to find the source of the mysterious noises coming from Sook and Tru's room. Truman came home from Nelle's one day to find Jenny waiting on the front porch with Queenie on a rope leash. Sook sat behind them, looking mighty sorrowful.

Before she could even open her mouth, Truman jumped into action.

"Queenie!"

Queenie bounded off the porch, the leash slipping through Jenny's hands. Truman fell to his knees and Queenie came running up to him. He hugged the dog and Queenie licked him all over his face. "Oh, Queenie, what would I do without you? You'll never abandon me like my parents, right?" He buried his face in the dog's neck, knowing full well that Jenny would never toss Queenie out now.

Jenny sighed. "Fine. But you must promise to take care of the dog and feed it all the leftover scraps we have and be mindful that it never bother anyone — except for a burglar."

"Yes, ma'am!" Truman ran over and hugged Jenny. She stiffened for a moment but Truman could feel her melt in his arms.

Callie, of course, disapproved. "I do hope you plan on keeping this mutt outside."

"No, ma'am. He's staying in our room, ain't that right, Sook?"

Sook nodded.

Bud was clearly in favor of Queenie. "Never had a proper coon-huntin' dog before," he said, petting the mutt.

"*Please.* Queenie's a bloodhound and must save his nose for more important things, like solving cases."

"Ain't nothin' more important than hunting coon, Little Chappie," said Bud. Still, he liked having Queenie around, and the dog became a member of their family of misfits.

Soon, Callie took to practicing her school lessons on the dog. Queenie was the only one who would listen to her.

12
Something Fishy

Nelle loved having Queenie around. No detective agency was complete without a bloodhound of its own. Now if only they had a case to solve.

One day, Truman and Nelle took Queenie for a walk. They were minding their own business, bored as usual, when they spotted Ed the egg man peering in through Mrs. Ida Skutt's window.

"Now, what do you suppose he's doing? Is he a peeping Tom?" asked Truman.

Nelle was not one to beat around the bush. "Heya, Ed! Whaddya know?" she said.

Ed looked over at them, concerned. Queenie suddenly started sniffing up a storm, pulling them up onto the porch. "Queenie, stop it!" Truman said.

Ed took off his white cap and scratched his head. "Well, yesterday I delivered eggs to Mrs. Skutt, and I smelled something downright awful. And now I come back and her eggs are still sitting there unopened, and the stench—"

That's when it hit them: the smell. "Golly, what is that stink?" said Nelle. "I think I'm gonna lose my breakfast—"

Queenie tore the leash out of Truman's hand and sniffed his way around the side porch. "Queenie, come back here."

Truman followed the dog and the smell kept getting stronger and stronger. Queenie rounded the corner to the back and became hysterical, yapping and jumping around like his feet were on fire.

Nelle tried to stop Truman. "Don't—"

"Could be the big break we've been wait-ing for!" he said. Nelle hung back but Truman continued around the corner with thoughts of murder and mayhem dancing in his head.

When he saw where the smell was coming from, he froze in his tracks.

Nelle was afraid to look. "What is it, Tru?"

"I think I found where the stink is coming from . . ." he said, gaping.

"Mrs. Skutt?" she asked.

Truman nodded.

"Is she . . . ?"

"Dead," he said.

Nelle wanted to run but found herself mov-ing toward him.

"There's something else . . ." he said.

"What?" she asked. "Should I look?"

"No!" He held up his hand. "I think she's been dead awhile."

"How can you tell?" She could feel her break-fast rising in her throat.

"Um . . . cockroaches."

Nelle tried to shake the image from her head. "What?"

"Cockroaches. Hundreds of them. Crawling up and down her legs . . . and arms . . . and in her . . . mouth—"

Right then, Ed the egg man came up from behind Nelle. "What in tarnation is that smell?" He turned the corner and came to a stop too. Then he busted out laughing.

"Great balls of fire!" yelled the egg man. "This is better than when Twit Tutweiler was struck by lightning!"

Nelle couldn't stand it anymore. She poked her head around the corner and saw what they were gaping at: not dead Mrs. Ida Skutt, but a pile of rotting, festering garbage topped with weeks of putrid eggs and coated with maggots!

The egg man couldn't stop laughing. "Well, she complained about the eggs going up a penny, and she vowed revenge. Said she would make a special delivery at our farm, and now I see why she was taking her time. Good and ripe. Oh Lordy. My boss is gonna love this one!"

Nelle wanted to take a swing at Truman for playing her, but she couldn't help but laugh.

"I had you going, didn't I?" said Truman. "You shoulda seen your face, Nelle Harper!"

She blushed. Queenie went over and licked her bare foot. "Well, if you're so smart, then where is she? Maybe she *is* dead, for all you know, trapped inside, rotting away, but no one can smell her 'cause of all this!"

Truman shrugged. "Good point. In that case, we'd have a new mystery, wouldn't we, Watson?"

They would have to wait for another opportunity. Still, Truman saw Queenie was a good addition to the team.

13
The House
of Mystery

The summer days grew shorter, and September, along with Truman's eighth birthday (for which his parents made a rare visit), came and went, but no big mysteries revealed themselves. Except for school. Truman began attending Monroe County Grammar School, but he didn't care for third grade, finding his teacher's attitude toward his braininess puzzling. Especially since that teacher was his cousin Callie.

"You're too smart for your own good," Callie said on day one.

"But how can I be *too* smart? Isn't that why we're in school, to get smarter?" he asked.

"It's those kinds of questions that make it hard for me to teach you anything," Callie said back. "An eight-year-old should know better."

Every day was a struggle. All he wanted to do was read stories or tell tall tales. But Callie gave him nothing but grief for reading too far ahead of everyone else and disrupting class with his wild tales about tigers or the exploits of his father the explorer, which she knew to be false. Every time he told a fib, she smacked him on the hand with a ruler. By the end of the week, his hand was usually bright red.

Truman began to dislike school because of all the headaches it caused him. Mondays were hardest because that meant there was a whole week still in front of him. So on Mondays, he, Nelle, and Big Boy took their sweet time getting to school, having little adventures or trying to scare one another along the way. Especially any time they walked by the Boulars' house.

The house was two doors down from Nelle's. Big Boy was certain it was haunted. From the outside, it sure looked foreboding and unkempt. Even on sunny days, it was downright gloomy, desolate and dark with the shades pulled shut, hidden by the shadows of ancient pecan trees that kept the sun away. Sometimes, Big Boy would cross the street just to avoid its gaze.

It was owned by Mr. Boular, who was about the meanest man in town. He never said hi to anyone. According to Nelle, one of his daughters had been killed by an alligator, and since then, the house felt more like a lonely cemetery than a home. Even though he still had a wife, a son, and another girl, *happiness* was not a word to use in describing the Boular family.

"There he is," whispered Truman one day. As usual, Mr. Boular was dressed all in black with a dour bowler hat and an umbrella. He was tall and thin and looked like an undertaker. He was walking straight toward them, his gaze absent, as if he were staring into another dimension.

"Say something," said Truman, nudging Nelle.

Nelle shook her head and elbowed Big Boy. "You say something."

Big Boy gulped. Mr. Boular was almost upon them. "Um, morning, Mr. Boular," he squeaked. "How's Mrs.—"

Mr. Boular passed by them as if they weren't there. A chill went down Truman's spine. It was almost like the man sucked the air right out of you.

"Sook says he's never said a word to anyone, ever," said Truman.

"How would she know?" asked Nelle. "She hasn't walked into town since I been born."

"He's a strange one, all right," said Big Boy. "But he's not the one I'm worried about—look!"

Big Boy pulled them down behind the rundown fence that surrounded the Boular property. Big Boy pointed at an upstairs window. Truman saw it—the curtain was parted and a shadowy figure was watching them.

"It's Sonny . . ." he said.

Sonny was Mr. Boular's teenage boy. There were always rumors floating around about strange goings-on, and they were all blamed on him. Sook called him Caw because of the funny crow-like noises he made to himself. People said he ate squirrels alive, and if you saw his eyes, you just might believe it. They were big and round and never blinked. It was rumored that he'd killed old Mrs. Bussey's black cat, cut it open, and stuffed it in a hole in one of the trees in the middle of the road. He was downright spooky—a boogeyman to every kid in the neighborhood.

Truman ducked down, out of sight of the window. "He gives me the creeps. Last night, I went for a walk after dark and I heard these strange cawing noises by this fence . . . *Caw! Caw!*" said Truman. "I looked through the slates and there were these doll's eyes staring back at me."

"No!" said Nelle. "It was Sonny?"

Truman nodded. "And he spoke to me! He said, 'Ain't you the nicest boy I've ever seen.' I started to walk away and he reached through the fence and tried to grab me!"

"What did you do?"

"I ran, of course! But then he called after me, 'Come back! Please don't be scared, I ain't gonna harm you.' I turned and saw him watching me and he looked so . . . lonely. I shrugged and told him I had to go home. Then his face grew dark and he started banging on the fence and hissing, 'Come back here or you'll be sorry. You'll be the sorriest kid in the graveyard!'"

Big Boy suddenly grabbed Nelle from behind and she screamed as only a little girl can. Truman and Big Boy couldn't stop laughing.

14

The Big Break

It was a Wednesday morning when everything changed. Truman and Nelle came
out of their homes like any ordinary day.
Except on this day, Big Boy was pacing about
on the road, bursting with excitement. "Did
you hear?" he said. "Did you hear the news?"

"Hear what, Big Boy?" Truman said sleepily.

"Somebody broke into the drugstore!"

Truman blinked, looked at Nelle, then back
at Big Boy. "Was anything . . . *stolen?*"

Big Boy nodded eagerly and added, "Someone smashed up windows at the school too!"

Truman's eyes lit up. "Do you know what this means?"

"Finally, a case, Sherlock!" said Nelle.

Truman smiled. "The game is afoot, Watson." He reached into his satchel, took out his deerstalker cap, and put it on. "Always be prepared, I say. Here."

He pulled out an old corncob pipe of Bud's he'd found and was about to put it in his mouth when he saw Nelle staring at him. He handed it to Nelle. "Dr. Watson smokes a pipe, I think."

Big Boy seemed disappointed. "Who am I supposed to be?"

Nelle jumped in. "Why, you're the inspector who never has a clue, ya big oaf."

Truman corrected her. "Inspector Lestrade is the most famous detective at Scotland Yard. *And* a worthy member of our squad." He pulled out his magnifying glass and gave it to Big Boy.

Big Boy beamed, satisfied. "More famous than Watson?"

Nelle rolled her eyes but Truman was gazing at the courthouse clock in the distance. "We have twenty minutes till school starts."

"Fifteen. That clock is always slow," said Big Boy.

Truman recalculated. "Then we must hurry! Inspector, lead the way."

Big Boy stuck his tongue out at Nelle and made a beeline for the Monroe drugstore, where they'd spent many an hour at the soda-fountain counter.

When they arrived at the scene, A.C. was already there. Dressed in a brown vested suit and horn-rimmed glasses, he was standing outside, talking to the bearded policeman about some broken glass on the ground.

Truman shook his head. "Looks like my brother, Mycroft, has beat us to the punch once more."

Nelle rolled her eyes again. "My daddy is

not your brother. That would make you my uncle and you're too much of a shrimp for that. Come on."

"I'm confused," said Big Boy. "A.C.'s your brother?"

"Morning, A.C.!" Nelle shouted. Her father barely glanced at her. He didn't mind her calling him by his nickname, but in public she should've addressed him as Father.

Truman took the magnifying glass from Big Boy and started examining the ground. "Morning, sir. Any clues?" asked Truman.

A.C. lowered his glasses and studied this curious boy. "You're Truman, aren't you? I've heard a lot about you. I hear you're the smartest lad in Monroeville."

Truman looked at Nelle, who blushed. Truman blushed too.

"I read a lot, sir. People say I'm mature for my age."

"Well, as long as you don't take after your father—" he said absent-mindedly, and then he corrected himself. "I mean to say . . ." He paused, looking Truman up and down. Truman certainly was the best-dressed kid in town. "I hear you're good with the crossword puzzles. Perhaps some Sunday, you could help me out. Those highfalutin words always get me."

Truman almost reached for his dictionary but he already knew the term Sherlock would have used in this situation. "Indubitably."

A.C. was a serious man, but he cracked a smile. "I'd enjoy that."

Nelle butted in, pointing with her pipe. "A.C., don't you know this is Sherlock Holmes?"

"And I am Inspector Les Trade!" added Big Boy, taking the magnifying glass back from Truman.

"Ah, I see. And you are here to help solve the crime, are you?" A.C. asked.

A.C. Lee was one of the best lawyers in all of Monroeville. When things went wrong, he was usually called in to give his expert advice. He slowly checked his pocket watch. "Well, Inspector, Mr. Holmes, and Dr. Watson . . . it would appear the real mystery is why you all are here and not on your way to school."

Truman pushed a piece of glass with his white shoe, then walked over the broken shards to stare into the drugstore window. "Were any items stolen, Mycrof—Mr. Lee?"

Mr. Lee sighed. "As a matter of fact, yes. Some two-cent candy sticks and a plug of tobacco—"

Truman took out the little notebook he always carried around to record his observations in. Usually, he wrote about how the sun filtered through the morning fog on the creek or described the smell of the blue hydrangeas that filled his yard.

But now was business. "Dr. Watson, take note. The criminal is clearly a teenager. A boy, I believe. Maybe two."

Nelle whipped out *her* notepad and started writing too. "What makes you think so, Sherlock?"

He turned to Mr. Lee. "A master criminal would have picked the lock and stolen money or linens or something of worth." He scanned the ground. "A boy might use something lying around to smash a window. Hello . . ."

He bent down and picked up a rock the size of a large marble. He held it up to the light, examined it, then stuck it in his pocket. "A girl might steal candy, but only a boy would steal both candy *and* tobacco," he concluded.

Big Boy jumped in. "Now all we gotta do is search every boy who eats candy and chews tobacca in Monroe County."

Nelle shook her head. "That would be every teenage lug-head who lives and breathes. We need to narrow down the list of suspects."

Mr. Lee cleared his throat. "Those are all very intriguing theories, but . . . there was one other stolen item: a cameo brooch."

"What's a brooch?" asked Big Boy.

"A cameo brooch is a pretty piece of jewelry with a carving in it," said Truman. "Jenny has one. They can be worth a lot of money."

A.C. leaned down and whispered, "But this one was special. It was an emerald-green brooch with a carving of a snake on it. The snake had red stones for eyes."

Truman nodded eagerly. "Excellent. A jewel thief."

"Maybe. Or just some kid who thought it looked pretty," said A.C. He pulled out his pocket watch and checked the time again. "Either way, children, you have exactly four minutes to get to school now. I suggest you mull over the possibilities on your way. Now scoot." He gave Nelle a gentle push, but she didn't go willingly.

"You'll let us know what you find this afternoon, right, A.C.?"

A.C. winked. "Indubitably."

Truman grinned the whole way to school.

15

A Rock-Solid Case

When they got within spitting distance of Monroe County Grammar School, Truman saw the broken glass by the front door. Callie and the other teachers were directing the students through a side entrance.

"Do you think it's connected, Sherlock?" asked Big Boy, looking through the magnifying glass.

"Just like a button to a jacket," he said as he

slipped into the line. Truman broke away from the flow of traffic as soon as Callie wasn't looking. He walked calmly over to the front door, where Hudson, the old janitor, was sweeping up.

"Morning, Hudson," he said, tipping his cap. He started scanning the ground for clues.

"Mornin', Mr. Truman," said Hudson, staring at his odd cap. "Sure is a mess this morning."

Truman spotted something on the steps among the broken glass.

"Hello . . ." he said to himself. He leaned down and picked up a small rock and studied it. He reached into his pocket and took out the other rock he'd found minutes before. They were about the same.

Hudson noticed the stones. "Jus' toss 'em over by the flagpole with the rest of 'em."

Truman followed Hudson's gaze over to a small rock garden around the pole. All the rocks were about the same size and color.

"The plot thickens," he said, rubbing the stones. "Thanks, Hudson." He ran over to join up with the others in line.

"Well?" asked Big Boy. "Any clues?"

Truman nodded, holding up the rocks. "What do you see?"

Nelle grabbed Big Boy's magnifying glass and examined the rocks. "They're . . . the same?"

"My conclusion exactly, Watson. Two broken windows on the same night? Any fool can see they're connected."

When Truman pointed out the rock garden to them, Nelle and Big Boy had to agree. "I would conclude that they struck here first, got an appetite for recklessness, and went into town for more."

"Ain't these rocks kind of small to break a winda?" asked Nelle, sucking on her pipe.

"Isn't a bullet small?" answered Truman. "The more important question is not how, but who."

"Who?" asked Big Boy.

"Exactly," said Truman. "An angry student? A bitter teacher? We need to find out if something was stolen from here too."

"Maybe the school has more brooches," said Big Boy.

"Maybe your brain is a brooch, Big Boy," said Nelle.

"Pay attention," Truman said as they approached Cousin Callie. She wore her collar too tight and it made her look like she was always about to pass out. She was not in a good mood, as usual. Keeping the children in line was like herding cats, and she disliked cats.

Truman tried to talk to her. "Callie, I was wondering—"

"Truman. Can you not see how busy we are? This unfortunate accident has put us all behind schedule."

"Well, about the accident, do you know who—"

"I am in such a state. *Get back in line!*" she yelled at another student who'd wandered two steps off.

"But, Callie, who—"

Callie grabbed Truman by the collar of his jacket and stared daggers at him. "Do. Not. Cause. Trouble. And take off that silly hat."

Truman, red-faced, nodded. Nelle and Big Boy stared at the ground and shuffled along.

"She's still mad because I can read two grades higher than her other students," he hissed to Nelle. "Sometimes, I have to pretend not to know things just so she won't look bad!"

"Go see if she'll talk to you, Big Boy," said Nelle.

Big Boy was not about to do that. Callie scared him.

Nelle crossed her arms. "I don't think she knows anything anyways. Maybe I will do a little detecting on my own."

At lunch, Nelle bypassed the teachers and went straight back to Hudson, the janitor. She had a hunch he knew more than he was letting on; he was often the first one in and the last one out at night. He must have seen something.

"Excuse me, Hudson. How are you on this fine day?" Nelle said, all smiles.

Hudson viewed her suspiciously, puzzled that two children would greet him in one day when most tended to ignore him.

She smiled at him with her big hazel eyes. "I was wondering . . . if you had an opinion on who mighta done this horrid thing to our school."

Hudson looked at her uneasily. He wanted to avoid trouble. "Well, Miss Nelle, I don't rightly know. From the way them kids is talkin', they think it's the boogeyman that done it. Nothin' stolen, just a mess of pecan shells all over Principal York's office. Plus"—he glanced around to see if anyone was listening—"someone drew a giant snake on the chalkboard."

"Another snake!" said Nelle.

Hudson nodded. "Strange goings-on, if you ask me."

Nelle's eyes went wide with excitement. "What'd it look like?"

Hudson shrugged. "It were too simple a

pitcher to tell what kinda snake. It just looked like a giant *S*. With pink eyes."

"Pink eyes?" she asked.

He dug around in his pocket and produced a piece of pink chalk. "Closest thing to red, I suppose."

Nelle was excited to report her findings to the others. As soon as school was over, she, Truman, and Big Boy met up by the swing set to discuss the case.

Truman grew excited as Nelle told him about the pecans and especially the snake drawing. "Those are two very important clues, Watson. It means that (a) the suspect has access to a pecan tree, since there aren't any here, and (2) he or they have something against the principal, and (c) . . . he must like snakes. Maybe they belong to some kind of secret snake society"—he snapped his fingers—"the Red-Eyed Snake Gang!"

"You mean pinkeye," said Big Boy, chuckling to himself. "My baby sister gave me pinkeye once."

"Maybe it was some farmer's kid?" said Nelle, unsure.

"What farmer's kid is going to break into a school and leave pecans behind? And why would he want a cameo brooch?" Truman paced back and forth. "And what does the snake mean anyways? Is it a warning of some kind?"

"Heck, everyone likes pecans. Maybe the brooch was a gift for his mom?" said Big Boy.

Truman ignored him. "We need to interview Principal York and find out who his enemies are."

"I don't think *anyone* likes the principal," Nelle said. "But who would play a joke on him?"

"Somebody who's either above the law or just playing a prank. In any case, we must interview the principal and narrow down the suspects," said Truman.

"And how we gonna do that? We cain't just waltz in there and start asking questions," said Nelle.

Truman took out his notepad. "We can if we pose as *reporters*."

16
The Usual Suspects

Reporters?" said Principal York, sounding skeptical. "I don't have time for this nonsense, children. Aren't your parents expecting you home?" The principal was a man in a hurry, eating a banana-and-mayo sandwich and, for some reason, trying on costume jackets.

"No, sir. We usually don't show up till supper's served," said Nelle. "What are the costumes for?"

"If you must know, I am playing King Lear

in this year's agricultural festival. And I'm late for rehearsal."

Truman saw the office had been cleared of evidence, so he plopped himself down on the big chair in front of the principal's desk and dangled his feet. "Perhaps you'll have some time for the *Monroe Journal*." He poised his pencil over his notebook just like a real journalist.

The principal eyed Nelle, whose father was, in fact, the editor of the paper. "It's true," said Nelle. "Truman won a big contest last year for a story he wrote. We're doing a report on the burglaries. We're junior . . . detectives."

"Detective-journalists," corrected Truman.

"We already know about the pecans and the snake, sir," added Big Boy.

The principal looked flustered. He knew Truman was persistent, and that arguing often took more time than playing along. "What . . . do you children want to know?" He smiled through gritted teeth.

"Weeeell . . ." Truman said in a long-drawn-out way that he hoped suggested he knew more than he actually did. "It's obviously an inside job. A student, I suspect . . . do you have a fear of snakes?" He watched the principal closely, looking for a reaction. Clearly the principal did not care for Truman's eccentric ways.

"Or of pecans?" added Big Boy. "Or of—"

"Sir," interrupted Nelle. Even though she had a reputation as a bully on the playground, she could be soft and kind when she needed to. "We're just trying to get at the truth. Do the students have anything to fear? I worry for their safety."

The principal sat back in his chair. "No, we believe it was just a childish prank. And no, I am *not* afraid of snakes *or* pecans. As for who played the prank, the students in question no longer attend this school, and that is all I can say on the matter."

Truman leaned in. "Then you *do* know who did it? Have any arrests been made?"

The principal waved him off. "No arrests

have been made, there's no story here, and it's against policy to release any names to the . . . press. Now, if you'll excuse me, I am expected down at the community theater for rehearsals!"

Truman, Nelle, and Big Boy walked quietly through town, weaving between the old oak trees that grew down the middle of Alabama Avenue. Clouds of dust kicked up by horse-drawn wagons gave a dingy look to everything, coating store windows and wooden porches in red powder.

"Well, *that* got us nowhere," said Big Boy glumly.

Truman would have none of it. "Inspector, to solve the case, you have to read *between* the lines. He seemed like he was avoiding the truth. Former students? Troublemakers looking to even the score, is more like it. I think Mr. York was hiding something."

He stopped suddenly in the middle of the road, his thoughts racing.

"What is it, Tru—Mr. Holmes?" asked Big Boy.

Tru turned to a dust-covered store window and wrote the word *suspects* on the glass. "We need a list of suspects. Who around here is always getting in trouble?"

Nelle didn't have to think long. "The boys over at Hatter's Mill, for one. Billy Eugene and all them . . . Hutch, Doofie, and that awful Twiggs Butts."

"What about Wash Jones? He's always acting suspicious," said Big Boy.

"*Blind* Captain Wash Jones?" said Nelle. "He's old. I don't think he ever went to that school. Oh, and he's *blind*, dummy!"

"It was just an idea," said Big Boy.

"What about . . . bullies?" Truman said.

Big Boy and Nelle looked at each other.

"What?" asked Truman.

"Well, there's um . . . Boss," said Big Boy.

"Why don't I know about this brute?" asked Truman.

"'Cause he mostly hangs out over in Mudtown. You don't wanna go messin' with Boss," said Big Boy.

"It's not worth it," added Nelle.

Truman's interest was piqued. "Why, what's he like?"

"He's the meanest kid in all of Monroe County," said Nelle. "He's only twelve, but I know grownups who are scared of him."

"Why, I bet he could eat three kids the size of Truman and still be hungry," said Big Boy.

"Oh, nonsense," said Truman. "One thing I learned on the river is that if you don't act scared, you can actually talk to anyone. I've seen all types of dangerous folks on that steamboat. Some of them turned out to be downright friendly."

"Truman, do you even know how to fight?" asked Nelle.

Truman took out his deerstalker cap and put it on. "One doesn't have to fight when one uses one's brains. I have an idea. Why don't you two go talk to Billy Eugene and his pals and leave this Boss to me."

"You're crazy, Truman," said Nelle.

"That's why I'm the brains and you're the brawn," he said.

"That don't make a lick of sense," said Nelle. "But if you wanna get the snot kicked outta you, be my guest."

17

*Bad Day
in Mudtown*

Truman wasn't stupid; he took Queenie with him. The dog had not yet proved his worth when it came to being a guard dog but he was better than nothing. Besides, Big Boy had told Tru that Boss smelled like a sweaty beast; maybe Queenie could sniff him out.

Mudtown was only ten blocks away from Truman's house but it might as well have been on a different planet. It was the poor section of Monroeville, where the black servants and out-of-luck white folks lived. Since the blight of the Great Depression hit, jobs had been disappearing left and right all over Monroe County. Even Callie feared for hers. Mudtown wasn't just a place on the map anymore — it was a feeling of despair and hopelessness that had been slowly spreading into town like a virus. Every day Jenny complained that more and more people had less and less to spend in her store. She worried that when people went hungry, they did desperate things.

Truman didn't care about any of that now. Wearing his little white suit and deerstalker cap and walking his precious little Queenie, Truman would have stood out in any part of town. In Mudtown, everyone he passed stopped to stare at him. But Truman wasn't scared. He'd seen all types on the riverboats: gamblers, smugglers, whiskey runners, cowboys. This neighborhood, however, wasn't anything like that.

The houses were made of used wood planks

held together by ropes and torn tarpaulins. People were cooking squirrels in pots on open fires in front of the houses. Their eyes looked deep and sallow; hunger lingered at every corner.

It was called Mudtown because when it rained, the streets turned into rivers of mud. Keeping his white shoes clean was proving to be a challenge, especially since Queenie liked to roll in the muck. But Truman was determined. Danger never stopped Sherlock, and it would not stop Truman.

Queenie froze in his tracks and began sniffing. The dog took off suddenly, dragging Truman along. "Do you smell him, Queenie? Do ya?" he said excitedly.

They rounded the corner, where Queenie froze and started to growl. Truman knew he'd found his man when he spotted an enormous scruffy boy three times his size holding another grubby boy by the neck. His meaty fist was raised like he was about to do some damage.

Truman pondered his options and decided that being direct was the best of them.

"Mr. Boss, I presume?"

Boss's gigantic head slowly turned toward him. The first things Truman noted about this monster of a kid was the mass of knotted black hair on his head, the snarl of his crooked teeth, and his beady green eyes, which were glaring directly at him.

Truman was at a loss for words. "Um . . . I'm investigating a crime and, um, narrowing down the list of . . ." Truman lost his train of thought, but unfortunately for him, he'd distracted Boss long enough for his victim to squirm free and vanish around the corner.

When Boss noticed his prey was gone, he clenched his jaw as if someone had stolen his favorite toy. "You shouldn'ta done that," he grunted.

Truman took a step back. "Oh, I probably caught you at a bad time. Sook always says never interrupt a man while he's eating—"

"Now I'm gonna have to straighten you out real good." He pounded his fists together to make the point.

Truman hated to fight. He also hated running away, because that's what bullies expected sissies to do. Instead of running, Truman decided to outwit the brute. He calmly adjusted his little suit jacket and said, "I can see by your stare that you wish to cause me harm. But I am here to clear your name, not ruin it. As Mr. A. C. Lee always says, 'Every man is innocent until proven guilty.'"

Boss took a step toward Truman, Truman backed up into Queenie, who cowered behind him. So much for an attack dog. Truman tried to remain calm; he reached into his pocket and produced some nuts. "Pecan?" he squeaked.

Boss gave him a confused look.

"No? How about snakes? You like snakes?"

Boss glared and pointed his big finger in Truman's face. "What do you know about *snakes?*" he growled.

"Nothing, just wondering," said Truman, trying to nudge Queenie in front of him. Queenie was having none of it and scampered off.

Truman kept backing up. "Does your mother like jewelry? Maybe with snakes on it?"

"You ask too many questions," Boss grumbled, backing Truman up against a shack, where he almost fell through some loose planks.

Truman tried not to panic—instead, he stood as tall as he could and declared, "All right, you . . . *you!* Should you choose to fight, I must *warn* you"—he raised his tiny fists into a boxer's pose—"that Jack Dempsey . . . *himself* . . . gave me boxing lessons!"

When that got no reaction, he added, "He's the world champ, in case you didn't know."

"I know. I just don't care," Boss growled.

Truman took a step sideways. "Oh."

Boss grinned and held up his fists like he was ready to have a go. Truman swallowed his pride, and then some. "Maybe we could just shake on it and move on to other things?"

"I don't think so, shrimp," snarled Boss.

"Hmm . . ." Truman said, slowly lowering his fists and racking his brain for a better idea. Looking into Boss's beady eyes reminded him of the encounters he'd had with water moccasin snakes back when he worked on the river. He knew that if you couldn't scare them off, you could dazzle them into submission.

"Let me show you a trick!" he said suddenly. Truman spotted a part of the road that wasn't muddy, cleared his throat, and spread out his arms like a circus performer. Despite his delicate nature, he had the body of an acrobat with strong and sturdy legs.

Boss waited for him to run, but instead, Truman executed ten perfect cartwheels right down the road until he was a good block away from Boss. He might have been a shrimp, but he'd also been the best gymnast at his former school.

18
Out of the Frying Pan

Truman wiped the dirt off his hands, surprised that his white suit had remained relatively clean of mud. Queenie was sitting there in the road waiting for him.

"Some attack dog you are," he said. He waved to Boss and took off running toward his neighborhood, pleased with his escape. Queenie followed on his heels.

He wasn't sure what he'd accomplished, but he recognized that Boss didn't seem like the type to steal jewelry. And come to think of it,

Truman was pretty sure Boss had never gone to his school—he would have heard of such a brute. What had he been thinking?

Unfortunately, Truman chose a shortcut that took him through an abandoned lot, where, because he was so lost in thought, he ran right smack into Billy Eugene and his pals playing football.

Nelle and Big Boy were nowhere to be seen. Truman made a mental note to talk to them about following through on their investigations.

The boys stopped playing as soon as they spotted Truman in his fancy white outfit. "Looks like this here mama's boy needs to get dirty," said Billy.

Queenie took off running again.

Truman threw up his hands. He would have to do everything himself. He'd handled these boys at the swimming hole, so now shouldn't be any different.

"Hello, guys. I'm conducting an investigation—"

The guys were not interested in Truman's investigation. As they tackled him into the dirt, he thought of something his daddy always said: "Out of the frying pan and into the fire." He usually said it because he was always getting himself into an unlikely jam—much like Truman was doing now.

The boys knocked the steam out of little Truman; he tried head-butting them in the stomach, billy goat–style, but to no avail. His last resort, as they pushed his face into the dirt, was to spout off with as big a voice as he could: "I'm as tall as a shotgun and just as noisy!"

Suddenly, the boys scattered. Truman sat up. He couldn't believe it; it had worked!

Then he felt a giant hand on his head and gazed up to see Boss towering over him. "Oh" was all Truman uttered before his punishment came.

"Hiya, sissy. Remember me?" Boss growled.

Truman knew his best option was to roll up into a ball and play dead like a possum.

Hopefully, this bear of a boy would lose interest and move on.

Instead, Boss treated him like a rubber tire, kicking him and rolling him around in the dirt. Truman let the pain drift away and thought of better things: That one Christmas he'd had with his mother and father where they didn't argue. He remembered a giant turkey and Christmas presents and his father talking about a new scheme that was sure to make them a lot of money.

Truman started to drift off when another voice interrupted the kicks. "Get offa him!" someone shouted, pulling Boss off Truman. "I said, *get off!*"

Truman wiped the dirt from his eyes. It was Nelle. She had wrapped her arms around Boss's neck from behind and was whacking him on the head and kicking him in the stomach with her heels. Queenie was running circles around them, barking up a storm.

Boss tossed her like he was wiping snow off

his shoulder. She went flying, landed hard, and then bounced back up, dusting herself off and preparing to fight.

Boss couldn't believe it. "You're a girl!" he yelled.

"Maybe I am, but I ain't scared of you, Boss Henderson. I beat up plenty of boys at school and I can beat up *you*." She spat into her palms and took her fighting stance.

Queenie growled.

Truman thought Boss almost cracked a smile. "Lucky for you, I don't hit girls. 'Cept for *that* twerp there," he said, pointing at Truman, who flinched.

A couple of old spinsters on their way to the market walked past the lot and gasped at the sight before them.

Boss threw up his hands. He'd had enough. "You're *both* losers," he said to Truman and Nelle as he stomped off. Queenie gave chase until Boss almost kicked him. "And your stupid dog is too."

"Takes one to know one!" said Nelle. She

realized the spinsters were still staring at her, muttering something about Nelle not being ladylike.

She ignored them and ran to Truman, who was still sprawled on the dirt. She knelt by him to help him sit up.

"What took you so long?" Truman whimpered.

Queenie came bounding up to Truman, licking his hand. "Queenie found me and I knew something was wrong," Nelle said. Nelle wiped the tears from Truman's eyes. "Look at you, such a mess, " she said. "I knew I shouldn'ta let you go alone."

Truman stared at his ripped deerstalker cap. "My cap." He sighed.

"We can fix it," she said quietly. "Sook'll sew it right up and make it good as new, you'll see. But from now on, we work as a team, okay?"

Truman nodded. Queenie barked happily. "Where's Big Boy?" He sniffled.

"Jenny spotted us as we went looking for Billy Eugene. One of her workers was feeling sick so she asked Big Boy to help out at the store."

"Some detectives we turned out to be," he muttered.

"Don't be a dope, Truman. Sherlock got into plenty of scrapes. Only difference was, he always had Watson by his side." She tried to wipe the red dirt from his face but only managed to smear it more.

Then she started laughing.

"It's not funny," said Truman.

She rubbed the dirt over the rest of his face. "You look like an Indian!" she exclaimed.

His eyes suddenly lit up. "Cherokee or Sioux?"

She squinted at him. "Shawnee," she said and knew that was the right choice. She gave Truman a hand up and they limped into the tall grasses, playing cowboy and Indian with a wolf dog for the rest of the afternoon.

For now, the mystery could wait.

19
Playing Hooky

The next morning, Truman woke up sore and feeling pretty sorry for himself. He told Sook he was in no mood for school. Instead, he curled up in bed with Queenie.

Good ol' Sook. She brought him cups of his favorite chicory-flavored coffee, even though Jenny always scolded her for it: "You keep feeding him that and he'll never get any taller!"

Sook may have had a headful of thinning gray hair but she acted like a child around

Truman. She listened to every word about his encounter with Boss and how he'd managed to escape. As usual, he embellished the truth. In his version, Queenie grabbed the brute's leg while he used his judo techniques and head-ramming maneuver to outwit the monster.

"Now you're just lying, Truman!" she said.

"I swear it, Sook. Isn't that right, Queenie?" Queenie barked yes.

Sook brought him leftovers from early break-fast, as he called it. Sook and Little Bit's elabo-rate breakfasts were a wonder any time of day: ham and eggs, pancakes, and pork chops (when times were good) or sowbelly with crowder peas, catfish, or squirrel (when times were bad), along with the usual grits and gravy, butter beans, sweet corn, collards, jam and biscuits, and boiled okra. Truman liked to tilt his head back and let the slimy vegetable slide down his throat.

"Now let's see if ol' Sook can fix that cap of yours. But I still don't understand why it has two bills instead of one," she said as she wandered off.

Truman was starting to feel better when he heard a knock on his window. It was Nelle, waving a copy of another Sherlock Holmes mystery, *The Adventure of the Stockbroker's Clerk*.

He opened the window and was surprised by the crisp autumn air. "Brrr. And why aren't you in school, missy?" asked Truman, delighted to see his friend.

She coughed in an exaggerated way. "Why, I'm sick, Tru, ain't it obvious?"

She crawled in through the window and snuggled up with Truman. They made for a perfect pair of misfits—he too refined to play with the boys; she too much of a tomboy to get along with the girls. And that was okay.

They spent the morning reading the book and drinking coffee. They considered new suspects and eliminated them, like Black John White (who slept in his clothes because he sleepwalked at night and had a habit of doing things he couldn't remember. But they decided he was too much of a nice guy to steal) and Ed the egg man (who'd never had a kind word from Principal York despite years of delivering eggs to the school. But he had too much to lose to do something so petty). Even Callie was considered, because Truman knew she kept a list of students she disliked (he was on it), and there was a possibility that she might want to set one or two of them up to get them expelled. But Jenny would have locked Callie in the attic if she'd toyed with such a harebrained idea.

When they finished discussing everyone in town, and produced no new suspects, Truman took another approach.

"I know what we need to do. We need to go to the drugstore and talk to Mr. Yarborough."

"You think he knows something?" she asked.

"People go to the soda fountain to gossip all the time. I'll bet he knows *something*. Maybe even who broke into his store!"

They didn't wait for Big Boy to get out of school. Nelle knew from experience that the truant officer usually gave up by noon—after that, it was safe to be seen outdoors. They decided to pay a social call on Mr. Yarborough to straighten out a few facts. The plan was to just sit there and chat away, enjoying an ice-cold Catawba Flip or a fluffy Cherry Dope at the soda fountain. Then, using their wiles and charms, they'd get Mr. Yarborough to reveal some crucial bits of information that would solve the case.

That plan was quickly scuttled, though. It turned out that Mr. Yarborough wasn't even there. Instead, his soda jerk, redheaded Ralph, stood behind the counter setting up decorations for Halloween. "What'll it be, boys?" He winked at Nelle, who sneered back.

Ralph was just an employee and none too bright, so there was no use wasting a lot of time on him. Still, he was worth a short chat. "Two cherry Cokes, straight up," said Truman.

"When's Mr. Yarborough coming back?" asked Nelle.

"Oh, he's away till Tuesday. There's a pharmacists' convention down in Mobile," said Ralph as he served up the drinks.

It was a slow afternoon, as most days had been of late, due to so many folks having recently lost their jobs. The place was empty except for them.

Truman tried to make small talk. "That was too bad about the break-in. Thieves have no manners these days," said Truman, fiddling with a paper jack-o'-lantern on the counter.

"Wasn't no thieves," said Ralph, looking around the empty store.

Truman sucked down half his drink until he winced—brain freeze. "No? Maybe it was some poor, hungry family? Sook is always taking leftovers out into the forest where lots of folks are rooting around for turtles or squirrels for dinner. It's a downright shame, I say."

Ralph spat into a glass and rubbed a spot clean. "Or maybe it was just some wild teenagers looking to have some fun, get some free candy." He stared directly at Truman, having experienced his fake-epileptic-seizures-for-candy scheme in the past.

Truman stared into his empty glass.

"What about the cameo brooch? That must have been worth a lot of money. Maybe some poor soul stole it to feed their kids?" said Nelle.

"That old thing?" he scoffed. "Probably just a piece of costume jewelry that Mr. Yarborough kept in the glass case 'cause it looked nice. I doubt it was worth two bits. It was probably just some kids, like I said."

Nelle nodded. "You know who did it, then?" she asked, as innocent as could be.

Ralph placed the glass on the shelf. "Know one of 'em."

Truman whispered to Nelle, "What did I tell you? More than one." He turned back to red-headed Ralph. "Sooo . . . who was it?" Truman squeaked.

Ralph grinned. "Why, I can't really say, kid. You'd have to talk to the sheriff about that."

"The sheriff? So someone *was* arrested?" he said, excited.

Ralph shook his head. "Didn't say that neither." He snickered. "More like . . . grounded."

"Huh?" said Nelle. "That don't make sense."

Truman put two and two together. "I see . . . well, thanks for your time, Ralph. Come on, Nelle." He tugged on her overalls, pulling her away from the counter.

"But I haven't finished my drink—"

He yanked and she went with him, taking a last slurp of her drink. But right before they stepped outside, Truman whipped around and pointed at Ralph's surprised face. "Quick—what do you know about the notorious snake gang?"

Ralph blinked and stared right back at Truman. After a good five seconds passed, redheaded Ralph shook his head. "Kid, you're too young for that action. Pit's no place for you two. Now git."

He walked out from behind the counter and

straight at Truman. This time, it was Nelle who pulled Truman away. Ralph glared at them as they escaped into the street. When they hid around the corner, Nelle was a little unsettled by what had happened. Truman, however, was rather pleased with himself.

"Did you see that? We got to him," he said.

"Truman, this is getting too weird. I wanna play a different game. How 'bout you be the cowboy this time—"

"What'sa matter? You scared—"

Before Truman could finish the sentence, Nelle swung him around and pinned him to the side of the building. Truman's toes were barely touching the ground.

"You calling me chicken, you little pip-squeak?" She glared into his face.

Truman knew when to back off. "I didn't mean nothing, Nelle. Honest."

She saw him turning pale and let him go.

Truman took a few breaths and straightened his collar. "You know you're onto something when you start to get to them. Did you see the look in Ralph's eyes? I wonder what the pit is. Maybe a snake pit?"

"I'm tired of all this snake talk. I don't like 'em," said Nelle. "I got bit by a cottonmouth once when I went swimming in Little River."

"Really?" said Truman. "I heard they can't bite you while they're swimming."

Nelle scowled. "Ask A.C. I had to go to the hospital and everything."

"Okay, okay, no more snakes for now. But we still have another clue to deal with."

"What's that?" she asked.

"Not what, *who*," he said. "The sheriff's son, Elliot. That's who Ralph was talking about! I never did like him. Or his dogs."

"Now, hold on a minute, Truman. Isn't Elliot the one that chased you down that time and locked you in the icehouse till you almost froze? You think he done it? How do you figure him?" said Nelle.

Truman shook off the memory. "It's elementary, my dear Watson."

Nelle threw up her hands. "What are you saying, Tru?"

He smiled. "I'm saying, who gets grounded by the sheriff? Only his son, Elliot, that's who."

Nelle slowly nodded in agreement. "Do you mean what I think you mean?"

Truman suddenly looked worried. "Yes. We have to go talk to the sheriff."

20
Showdown

Sheriff Farrish was a giant of a man who wore huge leather boots and a heavy black belt that holstered a pearl-handled revolver. There were stories of him shooting people who'd rubbed him the wrong way. Everyone avoided the sheriff like the plague if they could help it, but Truman knew Sherlock Holmes would never back away from a lead.

Sheriff didn't take kindly to Truman and Nelle waking him up when they knocked on the window of his patrol car. He was surly enough from the interruption of his afternoon nap but became even more so once Truman hinted that his own son, Elliot, had been involved in a crime.

He stepped out of his car and unfolded his body to the size of a giant oak tree until he towered over the two kids who intended to question him. The sheriff had one hand on his pearl-handled revolver, which just happened to be at Truman's eyeline.

"I don't know what you heard or what gossip people are sayin', but I would advise you to stay clear of the matter," he grumbled. "People who stick their noses into other people's business tend to get them cut off," he said without any humor.

Nelle was ready to slink off but Truman held his ground. "So, sir, you're saying it's *not* true?" He jutted out his lower jaw, trying to look tough. It had the opposite effect.

The sheriff just laughed. "It's true what they say about you, boy. You *do* look like a bulldog, though not like any bulldog I ever owned."

"Come on, Truman, let's go," said Nelle. Truman refused.

"Not until the sheriff tells us what's going on around here. The press has the right to know if there's some kind of cover-up, sir." Truman didn't know if his little ruse would work on a lawman.

"The press?" He guffawed. "Listen, you runt, if you're the press, I'm President Hoover."

Nelle started to wrench Truman away. "I'm a writer, Sheriff, and I'm going to write about this," said Truman firmly.

The sheriff spat a glob of chaw near Truman's white shoes. "Ain't no story here, son," he said, leaning over Truman. "Maybe it was the boogeyman who done it."

"Or maybe the answer is in the snake pit," said Truman, shaking.

The sheriff stared straight into Truman's eyes. "You look just like your mother did at your age. She was trouble too. Guess the acorn don't fall far from the tree." He turned and got back in his car. As the engine roared to life, he took one last look at Truman. "You too pretty for a boy. You wouldn't want to lose them pretty looks, now, would you?"

Truman gulped.

"Say hello to your dad for me, Miss Nelle. I'm sure he knows what you're up to."

He winked, gunned the engine, and sped out onto the road, disappearing into a cloud of dust.

21
Playtime's Over

Truman and Nelle regrouped in A.C.'s study. Nelle liked being in his room because it was filled with books—law books, religious books, encyclopedias, and almanacs. It was also a place where A.C. went when he needed to think—which was just what they needed, because Truman was *still* steaming over the sheriff's comments.

"It's just a game, Truman. Sometimes we're pirates, sometimes Rebel soldiers. Why don't we just start a new story?" asked Nelle, playing with her pipe. "Or, better yet, figure out what we're gonna dress up as for Halloween? My sister still has that ham-hock costume left over from the Hog Festival—"

Truman was rifling through his notes. "Isn't it odd that two people have mentioned the boogeyman now?"

Nelle shrugged. "It's just an expression."

"Or a clue," Truman suggested.

Nelle sighed. "Or just an expression, Tru."

"What about this snake pit?" he continued.

"You know I don't like snakes . . ."

"Come on, Nelle. You saw their reaction. Watson never gives up and neither should you. Even if you were bit once."

Nelle sat at her dad's desk and fiddled with his typewriter. "You're always making up stories, Truman. I just like to read 'em."

Truman stared at his shoes. "You're a storyteller too, Nelle. Just like me."

She looked at him ruefully. "Well, I feel more like a character in your play."

Truman swung her around. "You're the *star*

147

of my play, Nelle Harper. You and me, we're
. . . apart from everybody else. Nobody gets me
like you do."

Nelle nodded. She felt the same. She'd never
been one of the girls, and he understood what
it meant not having a mother around. Truman
was different but he made her feel like she be-
longed. Deep down, she liked being in his adventures, even if they got her in trouble.

Life was never boring with Truman around.

Nelle grabbed a blank piece of paper and
wound it into the typewriter. She stuck the
pipe in her mouth and poised her fingers over
the typewriter, then suddenly started pecking
away at the keys — *clack-clackety-clack.*

Truman peered over her shoulder as she
typed *Sherlock Holmes and the Case of the Red-
Eyed Snake Gang, a new mystery by Dr. Watson
(Nelle).*

"Nice title," said Truman.

Nelle took out her notes and began typing
up some of her ideas. Truman saw she'd been

scribbling away on her own. "I knew it! You *are* a writer, Nelle."

"I'm gonna be a lawyer like A.C. Go to law school and everything," she said without stopping.

Truman grinned. "Fine, have it your way. But when we grow up, I'm gonna find us a genuine case to solve and then we'll write about it for real, you'll see. You'll always be my Watson."

22
Little Bit o' Trouble

Not every home in Monroeville had a phone. Truman's and Nelle's did, and whenever Truman was too lazy to climb over the wall, he'd just call her up on the telephone. He rarely used his everyday voice; instead, he used his strange high-pitched lisp and told outrageous stories, or sometimes he greeted Nelle with a deep bass voice. "Hello, this is Professor Moriarty!" he'd boom — or some such nonsense.

Every house was connected by a party line,

which meant you could listen in on all the conversations on the block. Sometimes, just for fun, Truman and Nelle would listen in to hear whatever local gossip was flying around. And it so happened that on this particular day, they were each on the line and heard it click over to none other than that mean bully Boss Henderson. Where he was calling from, they didn't know, but he had to be close by.

On the other end of the line was a man with a voice like gravel. Nelle claimed it was Boss's daddy, Catfish Henderson, a scraggly bootlegger who was in jail more often than not.

"Meet me this afternoon at the snake pit," Catfish said. "Indian Joe done got a king and a moccasin goin'. We gonna make enough greenbacks to cover my hooch costs. And bring my hood, boy. We got fireworks tonight."

Truman and Nelle could not believe their luck. As soon as Boss and his daddy hung up, they both shouted: "Meet me at the secret headquarters!"

Nelle ran outside and made her way up to

their treehouse. When she poked her head inside, Truman was already there with his fixed-up deerstalker cap on.

"See, we were right!" he said, out of breath. "It sounds like there's some kinda secret snake society! Maybe the sign on the chalkboard and the stolen snake-cameo brooch were some kinda warning to others: the Snake Gang was here!"

Nelle considered it. "Maybe they sacrifice snakes to their pagan god and then Boss's daddy makes moonshine liquor from 'em."

"I know that Indian Joe fella makes whiskey—Sook buys it from him for her fruitcakes," said Truman, rubbing his chin. "Any way you figure, we got to go to that snake pit and find out more. You think you're up for that?"

Nelle sighed. "Do you even know where this snake pit is?" she asked.

"No." He brooded over it. "Maybe we can just follow Boss there."

"This is the same Boss who kicked you around like an old tire, remember?"

Truman nodded. "Maybe you're right." He thought some more, then snapped his fingers. "I'll bet Little Bit knows."

"Your cook? Why would she know?" asked Nelle.

He looked around and whispered, "Because she uses snakes for her voodoo."

Nelle did not like the sound of that. Little Bit worked in the kitchen alongside Sook. She was not little at all. She was huge. She was part black, part Cajun, and part Indian—"Little bit of everything," she'd say, and that's why they called her that. Nelle knew she had a dark past—she bore a thick scar down her face from ear to chin but never said how she'd gotten it.

One time, Nelle watched her tie empty bottles to the ends of the branches around their treehouse. "What're you doin' that for, Little Bit?"

Little Bit looked around, worried. "Spirits in the air, Miss Nelle. I puts a special potion in each bottle and it sucks the evil right up. Then I cork 'em and throw 'em in the river!"

Nelle did not like dealing with evil spirits. She sent Truman in alone to talk with Little Bit.

Truman wandered casually into the kitchen, where he found Little Bit frying up some catfish on the giant black and copper stove she called Ol' Buckeye. She was singing to herself while tending to the pan.

"What do you want, child? Little Bit is busy, cain't you see? And why you wearing that funny hat?"

He hemmed and hawed. "Well, you . . . use snakes, don't you, Little Bit? Do you know anything about the snake pit?"

She stopped poking at her fish and glared at him. "You been sneakin' Miss Sook's hooch, boy? Whatchu wanna know 'bout a snake pit for? An' what makes you think *I* know anything about that?"

"Sook says you're a voodoo priestess or something—"

She put her hand over his mouth. "Hush yourself, boy. If Miss Jenny heard you—"

"I won't tell anyone, Little Bit, I swear. I just wanna know is all."

She looked around to see if anyone was listening. "It's true, I'm a direct descendant of Dr. Yah-Yah, a famous voodoo doctor down in the delta lands. He were possessed by Damballa, the serpent god, who's the protector of the helpless. An' Little Bit knows what it is to be helpless," she said, feeling her scar. "Now, what do you wanna know, child?"

Truman gulped. "I'm trying to solve a case," he whispered. "I just want to know about the pit."

She shook her head. "I can see you one of the helpless. Is that for one of your crazy little stories? 'Cause a snake pit ain't for no kids."

Now Truman was getting scared but he was still determined. He knew she had one weakness. "Please? I'll take you to the picture show next week if you tell me."

She mulled it over in her head. "I don't like it, child, but I know if I don't take you to the pit myself, there'll be trouble for sure. I'd be fired if Miss Jenny found out I sent you to the snake pit alone . . . so I'll take you, but I won't be happy about it."

They shook on it.

She told him she'd meet him after supper down by the drugstore when she was done cleaning up. "And don't say a word to no one!" she hissed. "You always getting Little Bit in trouble. I just wish I didn't love them picture shows so much . . ."

23

The Smoking (Rubber-Band) Gun

The sun was setting behind the courthouse, casting an ominous shadow over the town square. All the stores on the square were closed for the night. Dr. Fripp's general store and Miss Jenny's hat store were dark and lifeless. Most folks were at home, sitting on their porches, reading the evening paper, or planning Halloween get-togethers. But not Truman. He'd told his cousins he was headed to the fields to collect fireflies.

The autumn chill was settling in; it was going to be a cool night. Truman drew his jacket tight and his cap down low as he hid behind one of the old oak trees across from the drugstore. When Nelle showed up carrying a couple of Mason jars, Truman made a quizzical face.

"To catch fireflies with," she said, like it was obvious.

"Don't you know we're on a mission?"

Nelle stamped her foot. "I ain't fibbin' to A.C. He asked where I was going and I told him we was getting fireflies like you said, so I'll do whatever you want, but after, we're gonna go to the field and get us some glow bugs!"

"Fine," said Truman. "But we're looking for snakes first."

Nelle spotted red-haired Ralph sweeping out the doorway of the drugstore and crouched down behind the tree. "When's Little Bit getting here?" she asked. "If Ralph spots us, we're cooked."

"She's coming. She was still cleaning up when I left."

"Why didn't you just come together?" she asked.

Truman frowned. "Any good detective knows you shouldn't be seen with your confidants. It's suspicious. Didn't they teach you anything in detective school?"

"Aren't *we* being seen together?"

"Stop asking so many questions," huffed Truman.

Nelle grunted and stared up at the tree. After a few moments, Truman saw Ralph go back into the store. "Whew, he's gone."

Nelle stared at the tree for a few more seconds, then glanced at the drugstore. After a beat, she looked back up at the tree again.

"Quit fidgeting, Nelle. People will notice."

"Don't you always say the answer is sometimes staring you right in the face?" asked Nelle.

"I guess so. Why?"

"Those rocks you picked up at the school and here by the drugstore? I think I know how such small stones could break such big windows."

Nelle pointed up into the tree branches overhead.

Truman squinted and saw a small wooden handle with a rubber cord attached to it. "A rubber-band gun?"

She nodded. "They musta been hiding up there when they done it."

Five minutes later, Nelle was hanging on to a branch about ten feet over Truman's head.

"You're almost there," he hissed.

Nelle was afraid of heights. "How come you ain't up here?"

"You're always saying you're a better climber than me—now, just inch out a few more feet . . ."

"There're ants up here. I hate ants—*oh!* I see it now." She pulled herself along on her belly until she was eye to eye with the slingshot. It hung off a smaller branch to her right.

Truman was keeping an eye out for passersby when he felt something small pelt him in the head. "Hey!" He looked up right as another hit him in the forehead. "What the—"

"Pecans! Someone was chewing pecans up here. I think we got our man. And from here, it's a straight shot at the broken windows."

She stretched her arm out with all her might and still couldn't reach the slingshot. "I can't get it."

"Well, try shaking the branch or something," whispered Truman.

She tried but that was hard to do lying down.

"Put some muscle into it. You're supposed to be the brawn, remember?"

"Easy for you to say . . ." Nelle got up on her knees and steadied herself.

"Careful," said Truman.

"Here goes nothing." She started bouncing on the branch, harder and harder. "It's moving!"

Suddenly, the branch snapped, and Nelle and part of the tree came tumbling down—right on top of Truman.

Nelle and Truman lay in a heap of branches and leaves on the dirt.

"Got it!" Nelle yelled, her fist popping through the leaves, slingshot in hand.

"Ooohhh . . . " groaned Truman.

Nelle crawled out from under the canopy of leaves that, along with Truman, had cushioned her fall.

She followed the groans and found Truman's face looking up at her. "Are you okay?" she asked.

"Next time, make sure I'm not standing underneath you." He groaned and struggled to get up. Nelle gave him a hand.

When he finally made it to his feet, Nelle showed off her prize. "Look what I got!"

"Let's see," he said, brushing himself off.

She held it up, trying to catch some of the distant light from the drugstore. They both peered at the slingshot. "Oh, my word, look!" Someone had carved a snake into the handle! The snake was shaped like an *S*.

"Hmm . . . just like the chalkboard. Whoever owns this sure likes snakes," said Truman.

"Who likes snakes?" a voice barked behind them. They jumped into each other's arms.

24
Into the
Snake Pit

Little Bit had herself a good laugh. "You two got the fear in ya tonight." She cackled.

Truman tried to act like he wasn't scared but Little Bit could see he was shaken up. "Don't worry, Mr. Tru, ain't nothin' gonna befall you now that I'm here."

"You just scared us—" Truman stopped. "I mean, you *surprised* us."

Little Bit eyed the broken branches. "What

in the world have you two been up to? No good, I suspect."

"We been detecting," said Nelle. "Look what I found—"

Truman stepped in front of her before she could show off the slingshot. "What are we doing here anyway, Little Bit? There're no snakes in the middle of town," he said.

"Plenty of snakes here, if you look hard enough," she said, reaching in her bag and pulling out some herbs. She stuffed them into Truman's pockets.

"What's that for?" he asked, trying to get away from her.

"Redroot and peppermint. Keeps the evils away. Something tells me you might need it tonight."

Nelle looked worried. "Can I have some?"

"Of course, Miss Nelle. Coming up."

Once she was done stuffing their pockets, Little Bit announced, "Now, come on, follow me and do as I says."

They moved quickly past the drugstore. Red-haired Ralph was cleaning the window from the inside and stopped to watch them go by. Little Bit ignored him and hustled the kids down the alley behind the store.

When they turned the corner, they came to a fenced-in area that used to be a stable. They peered into a hole in the fence and saw a crowd of men. They looked like escaped convicts from the chain gangs they'd seen along the roads to Montgomery. Hardened and shifty, they all smoked as they stood around an oversize dry-goods box.

"Stay close," said Little Bit as she herded them around back to the stable gate. Truman blanched when he saw who was manning the entrance: the bully Boss Henderson and his daddy, the notorious Catfish.

He pulled his cap down low, hoping the three of them wouldn't be noticed, but that was un-likely, considering he and Nelle were the only kids there and Little Bit the only black person.

Boss grinned at him; Truman didn't know if it was out of respect for their showing up or because he had it in for them. Either way, it didn't make them feel welcome.

"Nice hat, shrimp," said Boss, cracking his knuckles.

"We're here to see the fight," said Little Bit. Truman and Nelle exchanged glances. *Fight?*

Catfish stepped in front of them as they tried to enter. "You ain't allowed in here, auntie. No Negros, you know the rules."

"What about Indian Joe? He's as dark as me and you letting him in."

"He's got the snakes. You got snakes?" said Catfish, whose handlebar mustache, beady eyes, and sunburned skin actually reminded Truman of a catfish. "What would people say if they saw us cavortin' with the likes of you?" He hooted.

Little Bit scowled and turned to the children. "You still want to go in? You'll have to go without me."

Tru & Nelle

Truman nodded and stepped up to the gate. Boss grabbed Truman's collar with his giant hand. "Ain't it past your bedtime, midget?"

Truman's voice was strained. "I go to bed when I please. Besides, we're here to see the pit. How much is it?" He reached into his pocket and pulled out a quarter; Boss immediately let go and snatched it from his hand.

"That much. *Each.*"

Truman dug his hand into his pocket again and produced another quarter. Catfish grabbed it. "That'll do, boy. Just don't get too close now, ya hear?"

Little Bit frowned at the kids. "Go on, children," she said. "I'll be waiting here. But hurry back as soon as y'all are finished with your foolishness."

Right then, there was a sudden commotion. "Indian Joe is here," someone said. Nelle and Truman were shoved aside as Catfish and Boss and a few of their good ol' boys rose up to greet the man.

Indian Joe rode up on a black horse that had

168

seen better days. Joe was tall and dark, with leathery skin that looked like it hadn't spent a day indoors. Truman had never seen an actual Indian before, and Joe appeared to be the real deal. Strapped to his horse were two large cloth bags, both of which were squirming.

Joe surveyed the crowd silently, raised his hand, and said, "How." Then he burst out laughing. "How y'all doing, you crackerheads!"

Everyone let out a big cheer as Indian Joe grabbed the bags and slid off his horse. Catfish slapped him on the back, "'Bout time ya got here, Joe. Folks is real eager to get going."

Joe paused when he saw Nelle and Truman. He held up a bag in front of Nelle. "You kids like snakes?" Nelle covered her eyes, and Joe and Catfish burst out laughing again.

The mob crowded in as Joe and Catfish moved toward the big box. "Keep your eyes open," Truman whispered to her. "Maybe this really is some kind of secret snake society."

Joe handed one sack to Catfish and held the other one high for all to see. He then dramatically dumped its contents into the box. Truman and Nelle squeezed through the crowd so they could get a better look.

"A cottonmouth," whispered Nelle as it coiled itself into the corner. It was a big one, maybe five feet long. Just like the one that bit her.

"And in this cornuh"—Catfish held up the other sack, which was almost jumping out of his hand—"the meanest king snake ever to slink upon this earth. Now, who's gonna lay some bets?"

Hands shot up, coins and bills were exchanged, some folks shouting for the king, some for the cottonmouth. After Catfish's pockets were sufficiently full, he dumped his sack into the box and backed up a step. Everyone hushed up and leaned in.

Five minutes must have passed with both snakes coiled and eyeing each other from opposite corners. Finally, the cottonmouth made a move and the king rose up, swaying back and forth like an angry cat's tail. They stared each other down for the longest time, flicking tongues and hissing.

Indian Joe shouted *"Wooeee!"* and everyone jumped, including Truman, who almost fell into the box. The snakes suddenly lunged at each other and wrapped themselves into a squirming snake ball so tight, Truman couldn't tell which snake was which.

After a minute of tussling, there was an audible snap. Nelle gasped. The cottonmouth twitched and flopped around for a few seconds and then finally stopped moving. Half the crowd roared as the king unfurled itself from the other. It had broken the cottonmouth's spine.

Truman felt sick to his stomach. "Let's get out of here," he said as Catfish handed out money to the winners. Nelle saw him give a bundle of cash to Indian Joe and say, "See you after the meeting tonight down at the field behind the school. I'll be up for some drinkin' after some good fireworks."

Little Bit stood there shaking her head at the kids as they came out. Nelle looked white as a ghost. "Happy? Did you find what you was looking for?"

"That was horrible, Little Bit. Why'd you let us see that?" asked Nelle.

"Sometimes, taking foul medicine keeps you from getting sick," said Little Bit.

"What does that mean?" asked Truman.

"It mean, you shouldn't go looking for troubles when you ain't got none. Now let's git back home."

Truman nodded and took Little Bit's hand, but Nelle stood her ground. "What about the fireflies?" she asked innocently.

Truman sighed. "It doesn't really matter," said Truman. "Besides, it's too cold, isn't it?"

Nelle crossed her arms. "It's not cold. We got to go to the fields, Truman." Something was different in her tone.

"Come on, childs, let's get moving," said Little Bit.

Nelle grabbed Truman's hand and pulled

him aside. "That man said there's gonna be some kind of meeting in the fields behind the school tonight," she whispered. "I think it's part of their secret group."

Truman nodded; he knew a good clue when he heard one. But they'd need an excuse if they were to get to the fields. Luckily for Truman, excuses were second nature to him.

He turned to Little Bit. "I did promise Nelle here that we'd collect glow bugs," he said. "You can go home if you like; we'll catch up in a little while."

She narrowed her eyes. "I know spoilt milk when I smell it. No, Miss Jenny knows you kids is with me, so if you want to collect glow bugs, I'm coming with you."

25

Glow Bugs
and Pointy Hats

They made their way slowly through the fields behind their school. It was pitch-black and empty of people, the tall pines creaking from the wind that gusted across the tops of the surrounding forest. Little Bit stayed back, afraid that the spirits were roaming.

"Hear that?" asked Truman.

"What? I don't hear nothing," said Nelle.

"Exactly," he whispered. "Where's your secret meeting?"

They stood on the edge of the fields, letting their eyes adjust to the dark. "You sure about this?" Truman asked her. "They said they were coming *here?*"

She hemmed and hawed. "Well . . . maybe they had to go home to get ready. I mean, I heard what I heard, but maybe . . . I guess I coulda heard wrong."

The wind kicked up, blowing through the tall grasses, emitting the whispers that Sook called the grass harp. But it wasn't soothing to Truman this time.

"Spirits are definitely here tonight," said Little Bit, catching up to them. "Cain't tell if they're good or evil."

"Look!" said Nelle. "Glow bugs! They must be good spirits, Little Bit."

It started off with one twinkle, then two or three little streaks of light blinking on and off.

"Might as well collect some while we're here," said Nelle. "Then we won'ta been fibbin'."

Nelle handed a jar to Truman and made her way slowly through the waist-deep grass.

175

The further she got, the more the grass lit up, and soon she was walking through a galaxy of wispy shooting stars.

"Come on, Truman!" she yelled. "You need to forgit the case and come have fun instead."

She was right. Truman wasn't sure where the case was going anyway. Maybe chasing fireflies would help him see the whole picture, the way Sherlock played violin to relax his brain. "You coming, Little Bit?"

"Nah, you two go ahead. I'll just sit a spell by this here tree." Little Bit felt her way through the darkness to the trunk of a tree, where she plopped herself down. She was not used to all this walking.

"Okay, Little Bit. Start counting," said Truman. "Whoever gets the most, wins!"

They spent the next fifteen minutes running about, grabbing as many critters as they could. It was like trying to catch clouds—as soon as you were upon them, they vanished into darkness. But when one of them did catch one and got it into the jar, it was a victorious moment.

After a few of those moments, Truman forgot about the case and was actually having fun.

By the time Little Bit called "Time's up!" both their jars were glowing bright as lanterns.

"Looks like a tie," Truman said.

"Nuh-uh. I got at least two more than you!" countered Nelle.

"Let's ask Little Bit to settle it." They ran over to where she was resting.

"Miss Bit, tell this shrimp who won!" said Nelle. They held up both jars to her face, and she studied them closely.

"Don't count 'em. Just guess," said Truman. "Mine's brighter."

"Nuh-uh, mine is—"

"Hush, children. Little Bit don't guess, she knows."

They stood there as she counted, and the light from the jars made the tree behind her look different. The tree had lost its bark, for some odd reason.

Truman's eyes drifted upward, and he noticed all the branches had been cut off except for two big ones, which stretched out into the dark like arms. To Truman, it looked kind of like a cross. However, something else was even stranger. He squinted into the gloom of the night and when his eyes adjusted, he saw that the two branches were wrapped in white sheets.

He held his jar up high so he could see better. "Little Bit, why is that tree wrapped in sheets? And does anyone else here smell gasoline?"

Little Bit glanced up behind her and gazed into the blackness. A strange expression slowly came over her face. Suddenly, her eyes shot wide open.

"Children, it's time to go home." She threw the jars into the grass.

"Hey!" said Truman.

"But who won?" asked Nelle.

"Never mind that. It's late, too late for childish things." She grabbed their hands and started heading briskly back toward the light of town.

26
Blazing Glory

Truman listened to their footsteps tramping through the grass. He knew better than to question Little Bit. If she said move, you *moved*.

Little Bit suddenly stopped in her tracks. But the sound of footsteps through the grass continued.

Voices.

"What's going on?" whispered Nelle.

Little Bit leaned down into their faces. "Hush, children, come with me." Even though

Nelle could barely make out her face, she knew Little Bit was scared. *But of what?* she wondered.

Little Bit led them toward the darkness of the nearby forest. The kids had played there many times after school but now it just seemed black and ominous, the trees towering over them like phantoms in the night.

They didn't quite make it into the woods before the voices came upon them. "It's 'round here somewhere," said a man, out of breath.

Little Bit pulled the kids down into the tall grass; she put her hands over their mouths and held on tight.

"Found it," another man said. "Someone get me a torch."

They were surrounded by male voices; men tromped through the grass on either side of them. They ducked even lower and kept quiet. A man walked right by them, stepping on Truman's hand. It took all his focus not to scream.

Someone struck a match and lit a torch of some kind. "Now, don't go setting this field on fire, Frank. Just set this sucker ablaze and get us some light in here. Then the others will be able to find us."

Truman's view was blocked by Little Bit, but he could see silhouettes of pointy heads. He couldn't figure it. Someone held the torch high, and he saw the flames lick at the bottom of the sheets wrapped around the tree. The fire swiftly shot up the sheets and set the whole tree ablaze.

Only it wasn't a tree, it was a cross. And the men didn't have pointy heads, they were dressed in white robes and hoods with holes cut out for their eyes.

The Ku Klux Klan.

Nelle didn't know much about the Klan except that A.C. did not like them one bit. He said they were "the blind leading the blind." She had seen them march once when a black family tried to move into town. The Klan showed up in their robes at night and burned their home down to the ground before the family could move into it. Nobody tried to stop them.

The whole field grew bright from the fire; Nelle and Truman could see everything. There were about thirty of them, all dressed in white — except one; he was wearing a shimmering green hood and robes.

"The Grand Dragon," whispered Little Bit to herself, her eyes wide with fear.

Truman was staring at the man when he lifted his hood for a second to spit out some chaw — it was Catfish Henderson.

"Boss's daddy," he said. Truman glanced at Nelle and quickly realized he could see her. Which meant they could be seen by the Klan!

Little Bit slowly started to rise up, as if she were hypnotized by the flames. "Little Bit, get down, they'll see you!" Truman hissed. It was like she couldn't hear him.

He tugged on her sleeve; Nelle did the same. "Please, Miss Bit, get down —"

"What the—" said a man's voice. Nelle looked up in front of them and saw the silhouette of a man in a hood, holding a shotgun.

"Run for your lives!" Truman yelled.

Little Bit snapped to and realized what was going on. She grabbed the kids by the arms and ran as fast as she ever did. Little Bit normally moved in slow motion, but right then, with the voices and footsteps on their heels, she could've run across water.

Little Bit glanced over her shoulder at the spots of light floating through the fields. Men with torches, not fireflies. Truman could see the lights of some buildings ahead. Once they hit town, they'd be safe, he thought.

Except they ran smack into a barbed-wire fence blocking their escape. Actually, Nelle tackled Truman right before he ran into it.

They poked their heads up and saw a man making a straight run for them. He stumbled in the darkness, and the dry field around him erupted in a blaze of fire.

"Come on, children, we got to get outta here!" Little Bit grabbed Nelle and tossed her over the fence like she was a chicken who'd wandered out of the coop. "Now you, Truman!"

The wind kicked up and the fire spread quickly—toward them. "No, you have a dress," said Truman. "I'll hold the fence open for you then crawl through after."

"Hurry, Truman!" Nelle said anxiously.

He stepped on the lower strand and raised the upper one like boxers do with ropes when they get in the ring. "Go on, Little Bit! Quick!" She saw the fire coming, gathered up her dress, and crawled through with Nelle's help. They collapsed into a heap on the other side.

Truman could feel the heat on his back; the men were trying to put out the blaze. Truman scrambled through the fence as quick as he could. "Run!" he said to Nelle.

Nelle pulled Little Bit to her feet and ran for safety. Truman scrambled to his feet on the other side, but one of the barbed wires snagged on his clothes and wouldn't let go!

"I'm caught! Help me!" He could see the ashes and glowing embers from the flames settle around him. He had to move fast or get cooked.

Suddenly, Little Bit was standing over him. She grabbed him by his pants and tugged, but the wire wouldn't give. "Take them pants off!" she cried.

"But these are my good pants," he said.

"They about to be your good pants on fire, now git 'em off!"

Truman could hear the flames crackling behind him — he practically jumped out of his trousers! As soon as he was free, he and Nelle and Little Bit took off faster than racehorses out of the gate, leaving the fire behind them.

When they finally reached the school, Truman glanced back. No one was following them. It looked like the men were all struggling to put the fire out.

They collapsed behind a small shed to catch their breath. It took a whole minute for Truman to catch his.

"Think they . . . saw who . . . we were?" he said between gulps of air.

Nelle burst into laughter.

"What's so . . . funny, Nelle? I coulda been . . . killed back there!" said Truman.

"You shoulda seen the look on your face! You were as white as them sheets they was wearing!"

"Very funny . . . I seem to recall you screaming like a little girl," said Truman.

"I *am* a little girl, you loony bird. You were the one screaming—"

"My cap!" Truman shouted suddenly. He felt his hatless head and looked back at the field. "It must have fallen off when we were running. We have to go get it!"

"Hush, now, the both a you!" Little Bit yanked the redroot and peppermint from their pockets and threw them away. "I musta used the wrong mixture. We gonna go home now and never tell nobody of this night, you hear?"

Truman tried to argue. "But, Little Bit—"

She wouldn't have any of it. As she pulled him by the ear back home, all she could say was "Sweet Jesus, please never let me listen to this child again. I'm too old for this!"

27

An Omen and a Break

That night, Truman couldn't sleep. He kept Sook awake all hours, telling her of his adventures earlier that evening. The story grew into an epic tale of wrestling snakes and fighting off a mob of Klansmen, which Sook happily listened to. Naturally, he had saved Nelle and Little Bit from certain doom. But there was one detail he couldn't quite explain to her: why he had no pants on when he came home.

When he finally got to sleep, he had frightful dreams and tossed and turned until somebody shook him awake.

He was standing in the backyard in his pajamas.

"Buddy, you been sleepwalking again. Where were you going?" It was Arch.

"Daddy?" It took a minute for his brain to grasp that he wasn't in bed. "Where am I?"

"You're outside, son. You seemed awfully determined to get somewhere. Something about a rubber-band gun?"

"What are you doing here, Daddy?"

Arch smiled. "I came to see my favorite son, of course. I got this great idea that's gonna make us a fortune. I bought one of those steamboats we used to work on, but this one is gonna be like a floating theater. We'll have all the top entertainers, like that Louis Armstrong fella, and of course you'll tap-dance to his music, and we'll get Nelle's mother to play her piano—she's a fine player. But best of all, your mother has agreed to be our headliner—she'll sing!"

"We'll be together again?" asked Truman.

"It'll be just like old times. Won't that be swell?" said Arch, beaming.

Truman couldn't believe it. "What made you change your mind?"

Arch took off his hat and scratched his head. "Sometimes the answer is sitting right in front of you."

"What?" said Truman, puzzled.

Arch knelt in front of him and grabbed him by the shoulders. "Don't worry about it, son, everything will work itself out. You'll see." Suddenly, he started shaking him and, even stranger, barking like a *dog*—

"Wake up!"

Truman's eyes shot open and there was Nelle staring his straight in the face with Queenie barking and jumping all over his bed.

"Where am I?" he asked, confused.

"You're in bed, you loony bird, where else?"

He sat up. It was late morning. "Where's Daddy?"

"Daddy?" said Nelle. "He ain't here, I'll tell you that much."

"But he was just . . ." He realized he'd been dreaming.

"Last night musta shook a nut loose in your head. Look at this."

She shoved the slingshot into his face. "It's not a snake, it's an *S*," she said.

"What?" he said, still confused.

"On the handle. The carving. It's an *S*. What do you think it means?" she asked.

Truman pushed Queenie off him and examined the slingshot more closely. The rough carving had seemed like a snake earlier when he saw it in the dark but he had to agree, it looked more like an *S* now.

"Who do we know whose name starts with *S*?" she asked. "Sammy Zuckerman? Sally Randell? Um . . . Sidney Rae Mollet?"

None of the people she named were remotely suspicious.

Just then, someone knocked on his bedroom door. Big Boy popped his head in. "You still in bed? Sheez, some of us have been up since dawn. So what's going on?"

"Where have you been? You missed everything!" said Nelle.

"I been working on the farm like real people do!" said Big Boy.

"You catch him up," Truman said to Nelle. "I'm getting dressed."

Nelle filled Big Boy in on everything that had transpired in the past two days—red-haired Ralph, the sheriff and his son, the slingshot, the snake pit, and being chased by the Klan. Big Boy sat transfixed like he was at the picture show. He even took out a snack from his pocket and started chewing away as the story kept getting better and better.

When he spotted the slingshot on the bed, he got excited and shouted, "Smimphfrlop!"

"What on earth are you eating, Big Boy?" said Nelle, annoyed. "I'm trying to tell you we been working on solving the case, and you're chomping away like a squirrel."

Big Boy laughed and almost choked. He spat the contents of his mouth into his hands.

"Nuts," he finally said, pointing to the sling-shot. "Oh, is that a clue?"

"Gross," said Nelle. "Yes, it's a clue, maybe *the* clue. Didn't your mama teach you any manners?"

Big Boy grinned. "She did. But I kind of stole these, so I have to eat 'em quick!" he added, full of worry.

Truman walked in from the bathroom, re-freshed and back to normal. "Is he all caught up?"

Nelle scowled at Big Boy. "We're trying to solve a crime and you're *stealing?*"

Big Boy shrugged. "Is it a crime if you find 'em on the ground?"

"No . . . so why'd you say you stole 'em?" asked Nelle.

Big Boy looked around and came in close. "I snuck into ol' man Boular's yard and that's where I 'found' 'em."

Nelle's jaw dropped. "Are you crazy? That man would skin you alive if he ever caught you taking his nuts!"

"But they were on the ground where I found 'em! What does he care?"

They went back and forth until Truman stopped them. "Let me see something." He unfolded Big Boy's hands, examined the half-chewed nuts. "These are pecans," he said.

"Yeah, so?" said Big Boy.

Truman stared at his hands. "Hello . . ."

"What is it?" asked Nelle.

Truman was lost in his head, something the real Sherlock did whenever he was about to break the case open. "Now it makes sense."

He grabbed the slingshot off the desk and studied the hand-carved *S*. "Now it all fits!" Truman continued. "The boogeyman . . . the pecans . . . and the slingshot—it was there all the time, right in front of us! We have our *S*."

"Truman! What in the heck are you going on about? What do pecans have to do with any—" Nelle froze in midsentence with the look of someone who'd just found a gold coin in the street. "Ooohhh." She nodded at Truman.

Big Boy threw his hands up. "Well, for gosh

sakes, will someone please tell me before I lose my mind?"

Truman placed both of his hands on Big Boy's shoulders. "Congratulations, Inspector. You may have just solved the crime!"

28
Stakeout

Truman knew Sonny was inside the Boular house. All he had to do was talk to him and get his confession.

Truman, Nelle, and Big Boy staked out the mystery house after school, but they didn't dare get close. For some reason, Sonny's father, Mr. Boular, did not go to work as usual; instead, he sat glumly on a bench on his front porch, staring at the trees.

The sky was dark and gloomy—a storm was coming. The wind kicked up the leaves, sending the trio ducking behind Blind Captain Wash's fence. Since he was blind and deaf, they could spend all day in his front yard and he would never know.

Because it was Halloween, the Boular house reminded Nelle even more of an old graveyard. Surrounded by spooky trees and a rusty bent fence, the house was built of dark wood and was rumored to be haunted. It was foreboding and sagged in the middle like it was on its last legs. The yard was an overgrown tangle of scuppernong arbors and wild pecan trees. If you hit a ball into ol' man Boular's yard and he was home, you could consider that ball lost forever.

"I think he knows I took his pecans," said Big Boy. "He's just waiting for us!"

"Why would he be waiting for us?" said Truman. "That makes no sense. Sooner or later, he and his wife will leave and then we'll go in there and talk to Sonny and get to the bottom of this. Even if I don't have my deer-stalker cap."

That was Truman's plan. Exactly *how* they would do this, nobody knew.

"What about his daughter Sally?" Nelle asked. Truman just ignored her.

Hours passed. Mrs. Boular came out a couple of times and spoke to her husband. But he just continued to sit there glumly.

The trio of detectives passed the time playing tic-tac-toe on Captain Wash's fence with a pencil. They took turns on watch. On Big Boy's turn, he perked up when he heard a horse and wagon coming around the corner. But then he saw it wasn't a horse and wagon; it was Edison, dressed as a cowboy and clapping two wooden bowls together to make hoofbeat sounds. He neighed just like a horse too. Big Boy was amused until he started heading their way.

Big Boy ducked down.

"Who you hiding from?" asked Nelle.

The horse sounds grew closer. "Just some horse."

"You're hiding from a horse?" asked Truman. He popped his head up and saw Edison coming his way. Edison stopped as soon as he spotted him.

"Hiya, *Trooman!* Whatcha doing?" he said too loudly.

Truman ducked behind the fence. "Nothing, Edison. Just . . . playing games."

Next thing he knew, Edison was peering over the fence at them. "I like games."

Nelle panicked. "Get down before Mr. Boular sees you!" she hissed.

He spun around. "Where?"

She grabbed him by the scruff of his neck and pulled him over the fence in one haul. She was strong for a girl.

Edison toppled over her onto the grass. "Whoa! Is this some kind of Halloween game?"

"It's . . . a trick-or-treat game," said Truman, checking to see if Mr. Boular had noticed. Luckily, he seemed to be asleep on the bench.

"Look, Edison, here's how it is. We're hiding from Mr. Boular. He can't know we're here. You neither, okay?"

"What if he catches us?" he asked, excited.

"Then there'll be no treats," said Truman. "And we don't want that. So if you want to play, you're going to have to go and hide. Somewhere *else*."

Edison nodded.

"I liked your horse sound," said Big Boy. "You sure had me fooled."

Edison smiled. "What if I go hide in the barn behind Captain Wash's? Then I could still be a horse."

"That sounds fine, Edison. Just don't stay there too long. After a bit, you can return to being a horse and buggy and collect your candy."

Edison made a face. "I was a horse cart, Truman." He shook his head. "City folk . . ."

And with that, he stealthily disappeared over the back fence.

"Whew, that was close," said Nelle.

The afternoon faded and the sky turned to dusk as the end-of-day sawmill whistle blew. As workers headed home and children began to emerge in their Halloween costumes, Mrs. Boular came out to join Mr. Boular, and together, they walked down the front steps of the porch.

"They're leaving! I guess they don't want to stick around to give out candy," said Big Boy. "Speaking of candy, when are *we* going trick-or-treating?"

Truman and Nelle craned their necks up from behind the fence and saw the couple leave through the front gate and lock it. As soon as they walked around the corner, Truman stood up.

"This is better than candy, Big Boy," he said. "When's the last time you felt this scared on Halloween?"

Nelle was frustrated. "What exactly are we gonna do, just go up there and knock on the front door and say, 'Hiya, Sonny'?"

"We'll make it up as we go. Just remember, if he tries to grab you, run," said Truman. "I'm not afraid of him or anything, but you haven't seen him up close like I have."

They made their way across the street and over to the outer fence of the Boular house, slinking along like spies. No trick-or-treaters dared approach the place. Kids knew a real haunted house when they saw one.

Nelle felt some drops of rain on her arm. "Great, now we'll get soaked too."

As the rain started coming down, she scanned the grounds, looking for signs of life. They all heard the front screen door creak open, and they quickly ducked back down behind the fence.

Nelle peered through the slats. "There's someone on the front porch," she whispered. "Look, in the shadows."

"Maybe it's the sister?" asked Big Boy. He took the remaining nuts from his pockets and dumped them back through the fence.

Truman took a quick peek. "No, it's . . . Sonny," said Truman. "Look."

They wiped the rain from their eyes, peered through the fence, and immediately spotted Sonny, the spooky boy who liked to caw like a crow.

Sonny Boular was tall and thin and had a ghostly appearance. Once, Big Boy had seen him sharpening knives on the porch, and when he'd told some other kids, a rumor quickly spread that if you ever encountered him at night, he might kill you with a butcher's knife.

"Maybe we should go home . . ." said Nelle.

"Look who's afraid now," said Truman, trembling. "I thought you weren't scared by the Klan? Sonny's just a teenager—"

Nelle hit Truman in the arm. "Ow—what was that for?" asked Truman.

"For talking too much!" she snapped. "I ain't afraid. I'll go over there and interrogate the suspect now, if it pleases you."

Big Boy sat up. "You really think Sonny did it?" he said, a little too loud.

"I don't think, Inspector, I know," said Truman.

"Just because they got pecans?" he said even louder.

"Shush!" hissed Nelle. "Pecans, and everyone knows he wanders around at night, peeking into people's rooms. Besides, he acts weird all the time. And his name starts with an *S*!"

"Of course his name starts with an *S*! Why wouldn't it?" said Big Boy. "But he is weird, I'll give you that much. Sometimes, when I hear those stories about him, it gives me the creeps!"

"Who gives you the creeps?"

There was a flash of lightning and they all looked up to see Sonny Boular himself staring down at them. With the rain and wind playing with the shadows around his gaunt eyes, he looked like a monster.

"He's got a knife!" screamed Big Boy.

Truman and Nelle spun on their heels and ran so fast, they would've tied for first place in the Hog Festival hundred-yard dash.

They heard a scream rip though the darkness and skidded to a stop. "Where's Big Boy?" said Nelle, panicking.

A faint "He's got me!" rippled through the air.

Truman and Nelle ducked behind an oak

tree. "Oh my gosh! He's got Big Boy—what're we gonna do?" said Truman.

"We have to go help him," said Nelle, steeling herself.

Truman was beside himself with fear. "B-but what if he gets us too?"

Nelle pushed him up against the tree. "I thought you were a bulldog? Show me that bulldog face!"

But Truman couldn't bring himself to be a bulldog. He trembled like a Chihuahua.

Nelle shook her head. "Never mind, I'll go" was all she said as she took off back through the darkness to save Big Boy.

"Nelle!" Truman shouted.

She was gone.

The next thing Truman heard were scuffles and shouts. He shut his eyes and covered his ears. He hated fights and hated himself for not doing anything to help his friends. When he couldn't bear it anymore, he took off, running away from his friends and into the stormy night.

29
Caught

Truman showed up on A.C. Lee's doorstep, a blubbering, wet, out-of-breath mess. He was sure his two best friends were dead. The thought of being completely alone with no parents *and* no friends was too much to handle.

"Truman, what on earth is the problem?" A.C. said when he opened the door. "This isn't some kind of trick-or-treat thing, is it?"

When he saw Truman was seriously scared,

he brought him in and sat him by the fire. "Your knee is bleeding."

"I-I-I t-t-tripped . . ." Truman couldn't get the words out. "H-he g-got th-them —"

How was he going to tell A.C. his beloved daughter was dead?

A.C. knelt in front of him and said calmly, "Now, Tru, take a deep breath, then let it all out."

Truman nodded and wiped the snot from his nose. He took a deep breath and held it. When he exhaled, he barely spoke above a whisper. "Mr. Lee, your daughter is —"

Just then, Nelle and Big Boy came bursting through the door. "There he is!" she shouted.

Truman leaped to his feet and grabbed them both. "You're alive!" he said, tears coming to his eyes again.

"Of course we are, silly," said Nelle.

Truman looked at Big Boy. "I'm sorry, Jennings — I'm sorry I failed you," he blubbered.

"Shoot, Truman, I just panicked. When he grabbed me—"

Mr. Lee tapped his pipe against a bowl. "Perhaps one of you could tell me what on earth is going on here?"

Truman looked to Nelle; she sighed and stepped forward. "It's like this, A.C.," she said, and she proceeded to tell him the whole tale and their cockamamie schemes.

Truman sat and watched her tell the story even better than Sir Arthur Conan Doyle could have. Luckily, she stopped short of the part where she left Truman to go save Big Boy.

"What happened, Nelle? I thought for sure you two would be . . ." Truman gulped.

Nelle glanced at Big Boy, who blushed with embarrassment and said, "Truth is, Truman, I think I was so scared, I sorta, almost, maybe—"

"He fainted," said Nelle kindly. "When I got there, Sonny was holding him up so he wouldn't fall and hit his head. I didn't know what to say, so I walked up to them, and Big

Boy kind of got his legs back enough where I could help him myself. Sonny let go."

Truman sat with his jaw open. "But ... what'd he say? Did you ask him anything?"

Nelle gazed into the fire. "I didn't know what to say to him but he just stood there looking at me, so I think I kinda blurted out, 'Did you do it? Did you break them windas and all the rest?' And he just stared at me, nodded, and disappeared back into the shadows."

A.C. thought long and hard about their case. He'd suspected Sonny and Elliot and he'd pondered whether there was enough evidence to bring it before the judge. Someone should pay for the damages of the broken windows; that was the right thing to do. But to take that step and have them arrested, one had to be willing to accept the consequences. "Would you feel right if he and Elliot were punished?" he asked.

Nelle nodded. "Well, nobody told them to break them windas. Don't they deserve to be punished?"

A.C. paced slowly, like Nelle had seen him do many times in front of a jury. "If you do a wrong . . . you must atone for it, whether by penance or penalty or jail. But why do people do wrong? Well, that's a tricky one . . . you never really know until you consider things from their point of view. Until you can climb inside of their skin and walk around in it . . . Who knows, maybe they had their reasons."

Truman was confused. "Like what?"

"Well, that's the question, isn't it? Motives are a mysterious thing to figure sometimes . . . Did you ever do something that you later regretted? And how did you atone for it?"

Truman and Nelle took a deep breath and wondered if they had taken things too far.

30
Judgment Day

A.C. brought the matter before the judge. Neither Truman, nor Nelle, nor Big Boy knew what was said, for A.C. refused to divulge any information. But a few days later, Truman and Nelle saw Sonny and Elliot together. They were in the court-house, in front of Judge Fountain, a stern, gray-haired stone of a man.

Truman and Nelle watched the proceedings from the balcony. The rest of the grand courthouse was empty except for A.C., the sheriff, and Mr. Boular. An ancient fan turned slowly overhead, but Truman and Nelle could feel the heat this discussion was generating. Truman felt a pang of guilt as he watched Sonny sitting behind a table with his head bowed. He acted like a puppy that'd been smacked for chewing on the carpet.

Elliot was a younger version of the sheriff but he lacked the sheriff's cool. He kept interrupting the proceedings, saying things like "It wasn't my idea!" and "Sonny's the one who stole that brooch!"

A.C. looked at Sonny. "Is that true, son? Mr. Yarborough was mighty upset. He said it was a family heirloom but if it was returned, why, he might be willing to overlook the matter, as long as the windows were paid for . . ."

Sonny just sat there quietly, staring at the ground.

The sheriff sat behind them in the gallery, arms crossed. Mr. Boular was next to Sonny, his neck red with anger. He leaned over and said something harsh into Sonny's ear that just made him withdraw even more.

"Do you think they'll get sent to prison?" whispered Truman.

"Maybe we shoulda kept our mouths shut. It was just a few windas, after all."

"Maybe we could help pay for them," said Truman. "Set up a lemonade and boiled peanut stand here in the square. Why, I bet we could raise twenty dollars just like that!" He snapped his fingers, causing the judge to look up at them. He and Nelle slunk down in their chairs.

A.C. and Judge Fountain had a long conversation. The slingshot sat between them on the judge's bench.

The judge nodded, then sat quietly for a moment while A.C. headed back to the table. Finally, Judge Fountain banged his gavel lightly and said, "Will the defendants please rise?"

Elliot stood but Mr. Boular had to practically pull Sonny up by his collar. The judge spoke. "It is the opinion of this court that this kind of hooliganism in our proud little town should not be tolerated. However, it is also my opinion that these two young souls are worth saving . . . and to do so, I am assigning them to spend the next year away, interned in the State of Alabama's reform school."

Both the sheriff and Mr. Boular shot up in a huff and started talking out of turn to the judge. The judge banged his gavel; A.C. tried to calm them.

In the ruckus, Sonny's eyes drifted around the chamber. He was clearly wishing he were anywhere else but here. His gaze finally settled on the balcony. When Truman and Nelle saw he'd spotted them, they just sat there, unsure what to do.

Sonny waved at them until his father got his attention again.

"Come on, let's get out of here," said Truman.

They headed back to Nelle's house without speaking and waited in A.C.'s office for him to return. It took almost an hour.

"Well, what happened, A.C.?" Nelle asked as soon as the door opened. "Did Sonny confess to stealing that cameo brooch?"

A.C. took his time cleaning his pipe and tapping it on an ashtray. "No, he did not, Nelle. So it remains . . . a mystery. But both the sheriff and Mr. Boular managed to convince the judge that keeping them home under house arrest would be a far worse punishment than sending them away to any reform school. Knowing them, I'm sure that's true. Mr. Boular in particular insisted that Sonny would be taught a lesson he'd never forget."

Truman looked at Nelle and gulped. "Maybe we should help pay for the broken window," said Truman. "We could ask Jenny to give Mr. Yarborough her brooch . . ."

"Now, why would you want to do that?" asked A.C.

"'Cause it was our fault that Sonny was caught," said Nelle.

"Sometimes, justice is served in ways that make nobody happy. But I think they learned their lesson." A.C. nodded thoughtfully. "And maybe there's a lesson you two can take away from this as well."

Nelle asked, "What's that, Daddy?"

A.C. smiled and puffed on his pipe. "Stay here, children," he said, abruptly leaving the room.

"Where's he going?" whispered Truman.

Nelle shrugged. "Search me."

They heard A.C. open the basement door and thump down the steps.

"Doesn't he keep his gun down there?" asked Truman, worried.

Nelle slapped him upside the head. "A.C. don't know how to shoot. He's a lawyer, for gosh sakes."

They heard a muffled "Aha . . . there you are" come from down below. There was some rummaging about, followed by a few grunts, and, finally, the sound of A.C. plodding heavily back upstairs.

He barged through the door, back first, and slowly turned around. He held an old dusty metal box with a wooden handle, which he placed carefully on the desk in front of them.

Truman looked at Nelle as A.C. undid the latch. He opened it and revealed something that looked like an accordion on its back. But it was, in fact, an old black Underwood #5 typewriter.

"I learned how to write on this typewriter," he said wistfully. "Now I'm giving it to both of you. Maybe it'll be a reminder that perhaps you're better off typing your tall tales, rather than getting into other people's business. Leave that to the likes of me and the law."

Nelle jumped up and felt the keys. "Our very own typewriter?" she asked.

"Yes." He nodded. "Now you can write your own stories. Who knows—maybe that'll take you somewhere other than the courthouse."

Truman grinned. Christmas had just come early.

31
Writers and Beauty Queens

For days and weeks and months after, Truman and Nelle met up to write stories. One day, they'd write in A.C.'s office, Truman dictating and Nelle typing. Other days, they'd meet at Truman's, and he'd be at the keyboard with Nelle making up stories. Sometimes they met halfway, hauling that typewriter up into their secret headquarters (not an easy trick, but they devised a rope-and-pulley system to do it). Usually Truman had to pressure Nelle into writing, but once she got going, she was good. Big Boy wanted to join in, but he really didn't have the imagination for that kind of thing. Instead, he often sat nearby with Queenie on his lap, listening to the stories they wove.

And what stories they were. Mysteries and crime tales featuring themselves as detectives. Or adventure stories where they'd travel to exotic locales and get mixed up in intrigue and high jinks. Or just simple stories about busybodies in town who got into trouble by spreading gossip and rumors.

Truman was very protective of their stories. He kept them locked up in a trunk under his bed and wore the key on a chain around his neck. On cold nights when snow dusted the street in front of the house, he would recount a story in front of the fire as if it were true. Jenny and Callie didn't care for his fibbing but they found themselves laughing just as hard as Bud did at Truman's anecdotes. He told stories about Sook on Thanksgiving and Christmas that made her teary-eyed, and he saved his wildest yarns for New Year's Eve.

After the New Year, Nelle's mother came back unexpectedly, recuperated after her time away. In moments of quiet, Nelle would tell her some of their tales—mostly funny stories and mysteries, anything to keep her mind off her troubles. She listened attentively, trying to guess (and usually getting it wrong) what the punch line would be or who the culprit was. She enjoyed this, liked it much better than being in the hospital, especially when A.C. joined them for a listen.

The kids were having fun, racing home from school with new ideas. Monroeville was still boring, but at least they were able to live their adventures on the page, which was the next best thing.

Nelle's mother was not the only one to show up unexpectedly. One day, Truman and Nelle were cleaning up his precious Tri-Motor plane when Truman looked up and saw his own mother standing in the doorway.

It had been many months since she'd visited. He'd almost forgotten he had a mother. But seeing her in the flesh brought all his feelings rushing back into his head. He ran up and hugged her around the waist.

"I have a surprise for you," she said.

"What?" he asked.

She pulled an award certificate from behind her back. "Aren't you proud of your mother?" she said, showing it off.

"What is *that?*" he asked.

"Well, it's a prize that I won!" she said.

Truman and Nelle gazed at the award. It said *Elizabeth Arden Beauty Contest, First Prize: Lillie Mae Persons.*

"You won a beauty contest?" Truman asked, confused.

"I just sent in my photo and they picked little old me." She blushed.

"Who's Elizabeth Arden?" asked Nelle.

"Only one of the wealthiest women in the world who just happens to own the biggest cosmetics company in the States," she said. "And they've invited *me* to come up to New York City and enroll in a free beauty course. New York! Can you beat that?"

Truman looked depressed. "So . . . you're moving?"

"Oh, don't be a fuddy-duddy, Truman. This is your mother's big chance. I'll be back in a couple months. Be happy for me for once, dear. You can say your mother's a beauty queen."

"I think you're pretty, Lillie Mae," said Nelle.

"Why, thank you, Nelle. And when I come back, I'll do a makeover on you," she said, looking at Nelle's dirty hands and feet. "Heaven knows you need one."

She left without giving Truman a hug. He looked downright grim.

32
Reprieve

In the cold dampness of February, Truman was lying in bed, restless. He tried to sleep but all he could think about was his mother in New York. He imagined her all dolled up and walking down a fashion-show runway under the gaze of cameras and flashbulbs.

He heard the telephone ringing.

Truman listened as Cousin Jenny came down the stairs to the hall phone. He could faintly hear her talking but couldn't make out any words. There was a long silence, then he heard footsteps in the hallway. Finally, his door opened and Jenny poked her head in.

Truman pretended to be asleep. She crept slowly up to his bed and nudged his shoulder. "Truman," she whispered. "It's your father."

Truman opened his eyes. "Daddy?" Why was he calling?

Truman rubbed his eyes as Jenny led him to the phone. She handed him the receiver, but he wasn't sure he wanted to talk.

"Go on, Truman."

Truman took the call. "Hello?"

"Truman!" Arch's voice sounded far away.

"Where are you?"

". . . On the road . . ." His answer was garbled by the static.

"Where?"

"Truman, I need you to pack your bags. I'll be there in the morning."

Truman couldn't believe what he was hearing. "Where are we going?"

"A little father-son adventure. I think you're

old enough to see . . ." Again, the words were lost.

"A trip? Tomorrow? What about school?"

"School can wait. Time alone with my son is more important, especially since your mother—"

The line went dead. "Hello?"

Truman handed the receiver back to Jenny. She listened but there was nothing more. "What'd he say?" she asked.

"I think he wants to go on a trip with me. Tomorrow."

Jenny shook her head and put down the receiver. "I don't know, Truman."

"Please? It'll probably be for only a few days. And Callie could give me some homework to do on the road."

She sighed. "Well, I can't stop you. He is your father."

Truman beamed and ran back to his room. He went rummaging under his bed for a suitcase.

Sook woke up, of course. "For goodness' sake—what are you doing, Truman? It's the middle of the night."

"Looking for my suitcase. I'm going on a trip with Arch."

There was a long silence. "You're missing school?"

"Callie will catch me up—gotcha!" Truman pulled out the same old brown suitcase he'd come to Monroeville with.

As soon as Sook heard Arch wasn't coming till tomorrow, she went back to sleep, willing to deal with it in the morning. But Truman was wide awake now. He stayed up all night, packing clothes and making a list of things they would talk about while driving. He imagined maybe they would go up to New York to see Mother. Or get back on the steamboat like old times. Either way, it would be a grand adventure.

When the sun came up, Truman was exhausted but dressed and ready. Little Bit found him sitting on the stoop of the front porch as she came in. "And where are you going, Mr. Truman?"

Truman yawned. "On a trip with Arch!"

Little Bit rolled her eyes. "Don't get into it," she mumbled to herself. She smiled and went inside.

Nelle and Big Boy stopped by on their way to school. "Well, come on, Truman, we're gonna be late," Nelle said.

"I'm not going. I'm going on a trip. With Arch."

Nelle grimaced. "Where you headed?"

"Wherever the wind takes us."

"Lordy, help me," she said under her breath.

Big Boy just smiled and pulled her away. "Sounds great, Truman. I guess we'll see you when you get back."

Callie dropped a stack of homework on the porch next to him. "Who takes his child out of school for no good reason . . ." was all she said as she headed out.

Truman didn't care what anyone said. He was going to have fun. He sat there and watched the horse carts carrying deliveries from the underwear factory nearby. He watched the cooks and handymen walk to work from Mudtown. He watched the schoolchildren come and go.

Sook found him asleep on the porch several hours later. She picked him up and put him to bed.

Archulus Persons never showed up.

33

Banished

Many more months passed, and life in Monroeville continued at its slow but steady pace. Spring came, with Nelle's birthday and the flowering of blue hydrangeas and King Alfred daffodils, followed by summer and its oppressive, wilting heat. Truman's Tri-Motor plane mysteriously disappeared one day and was found wrecked by the roadside. Somehow Big Boy was able to rebuild it so it looked almost like new, despite the broken arm that he'd somehow acquired. But that's another story.

Truman and Nelle continued to write and share tall tales and enjoyed not having to go to school. When Truman's ninth birthday rolled around, in September, and neither Lillie Mae nor Arch appeared for the birthday dinner, Nelle knew something was up. There were rumors of divorce, but nobody, especially Truman, ever spoke of it.

One day, shortly after that, Truman didn't show up in class, nor was he at the treehouse afterward. Nelle went looking for him and found Sook sitting in the backyard hugging Queenie. Instead of being her usual happy self, she was crying.

"What's the matter, Sook?"

Sook wiped her eyes with her apron. "Oh, Nelle. We're gonna lose him." She moaned. "This'll kill him for sure . . ."

A chill went down Nelle's spine. "Lose who?"

"My little Truman . . . what am I going to do

without him, Miss Nelle?" Tears flowed as she petted Queenie.

Nelle couldn't believe her ears. "*What? Truman's . . . dying?*"

Sook shook her head. "No, Miss Nelle. *Worse.* Our Tru has to go to boarding school after Halloween. His mama's getting remarried and wants him to move to New York!"

Nelle blinked. "He's moving?"

Sook nodded and buried her face in her hands. Nelle refused to believe it. She raced into the house to Truman's room, where she found him in bed, staring out the window.

"Is it true?" she asked. She almost couldn't breathe waiting for his answer.

"Yes," he whispered. "I am dying." He feigned his tragic demise until Nelle came over and punched him in the shoulder.

"You're leaving me?"

He rubbed his shoulder. "That hurt . . ." he muttered. "And, yes, Mother has sent for me. She met a new man, Joe Capote, and she wants me to come to New York to live with them."

"Sook said you were going to boarding school."

Truman kept staring out the window, his mind working. "No. Unfortunately, they couldn't find one that would take a kid as smart as me. So I will live with Mother and learn only by reading books from now on."

"You're such a liar," she said and then immediately regretted it. Nelle still couldn't believe he was leaving, but the sadness in his eyes was real. She decided to cheer him up. "I can't believe you are going to the big city. Isn't that what you always wanted? To live with your mother, where all the action is? Think of the grand balls they have up there, the parties and the shows. Why, there'll be plenty of gangsters and nefarious deeds going on to write about!"

Truman frowned. "Yes, all that's true, I suppose. But I don't really want to leave here."

Nelle would have none of it. "Nonsense. There's nothing happening down here. There's no nightlife, no social scene that the papers write about. You'll be living the real thing. Think of all the stories!"

Truman rolled over in bed, facing away from her. "But I won't have you," he whimpered.

Nelle's heart broke in two but she knew she had to be the stronger person. She sat next to him, putting her hand on his shoulder. "Ouch," he said and she pulled her hand away.

He grabbed it and held on. "It's not my shoulder that hurts," he said.

She sighed. "You'll make new friends up there. Everyone likes you, Tru." She barely got it out before her voice cracked.

"You and I both know nobody likes me. I talk funny and I dress too fine," he said. "I'm a curiosity around here and you know it. People only like me when I tell my stories. I'm just a court jester to them."

"Well, so what if that's true? That's enough. Plenty of people wish they could tell a story as good as you. You'll be a great writer one day, Tru. And everyone will read your books and love you for them."

Truman perked up. "Do you really think so?" he squeaked.

"I know so." She nodded.

He thought about it, letting the images churn in his head. "I'll make you a deal: I'll write, but only if you promise to write as well. Then we can mail each other our stories," he said, hopeful.

Nelle didn't have the gift that Truman had, but she knew she had a good tale — or two — inside her. "You won't even care about me after a few years, Truman. You'll be so famous you won't have time to write to me. You'll be the hit of New York, going to big costume parties with anybody who's anybody, and you'll be all over the society pages in the newspaper —"

Truman suddenly sat up. "That's it!"

"What?" asked Nelle.

"If I have to leave, why, we'll just have to throw the biggest going-away party Monroeville has ever seen. It'll be a real humdinger!"

"Really?" said Nelle.

"I'll throw such a party, they'll never forget

me. And every time you show a postcard from me around, people will say, 'Do you remember Truman's Halloween party? What a night! I'll never forget it!'"

Nelle smiled. That was a fine idea.

34
The Last Hurrah

Truman would be leaving around Thanksgiving, so he, Nelle, and Big Boy spent the next afternoon after school concocting a party so magnificent, people would remember it for a hundred years.

The first idea Truman had was to make it, of course, a Halloween party. Since they had missed celebrating last year, the motion was immediately approved. The second idea he had was to have it on a Friday night.

"But no nine-year-old has a party at night," said Big Boy.

"Exactly," said Truman. "That'll make it memorable by itself. Besides, who wants to have a Halloween party in the day?"

"Oh!" said Nelle. "If it's a real Halloween party, then we'll all get to wear costumes!"

Truman laughed. "Of course, silly. It'll be a masquerade ball! Everyone will be required to dress up, even the adults! And we'll have a big contest for best costume and I'll be the judge."

"What about us?" asked Big Boy.

"Well . . ." Truman scratched his head. "How will you win best prize if you're a judge?"

Big Boy hadn't thought of that. "Will there be candy?" he asked.

"Of course! The winner will get . . . chocolate! As much as he can eat!"

Big Boy was already drooling. "Oh, I wanna dress up, then. Can we do bobbing for apples too?"

"Yes! And bobbing for apples too!"

"What about," Nelle said, "building a ride for your Tri-Motor airplane?"

Truman hemmed and hawed. His precious Ford Tri-Motor airplane was his most prized possession, especially after it had been wrecked and rebuilt. He was willing to let Big Boy and Nelle ride it, but *everyone?*

Truman sighed. "Well . . . okay, I guess I could ask Bud if he can build us a ramp . . ." he said, his imagination percolating. "Maybe the ramp could shoot down the back steps from the porch. And then the plane will build up so much speed, it'll actually . . . start to fly!" Nelle and Big Boy cheered.

"This'll be the best party ever!" said Nelle.

"Of course, we'll need Jenny on our side," he said. "I don't think she's ever had a party here, let alone the biggest party Monroeville has ever seen."

"Well, the adults can have their own party, in the living room," said Big Boy. "They can drink punch and listen to her Victrola record player."

"That's a swell idea, Big Boy."

"Why, Jenny can invite the most important people in town . . . maybe even the mayor," said Nelle.

Truman had stars in his eyes. He could see it all—a hundred kids and adults having the time of their lives. They would set up a carnival in the backyard, complete with circus acts and games of all kinds. "Queenie can dress up as a circus dog and I'll get Black John White and Little Bit to perform!"

Black John had a white suit and hat that Bud had given him for a gift out of gratitude for all the years he'd worked for him. He wore it only inside his shack on his wedding anniversary. Nobody had ever seen him in it except Truman, who'd walked in on John and his wife by accident. Truman thought that with a little white makeup, Black John would look just like a fancy ghost.

Aside from being a voodoo priestess, Little Bit also on occasion sat on the porch and played an accordion her father had left her when he passed. She too could dress up like one of the spirits she was always going on about. (Later, when Little Bit had her doubts, Truman reminded her that on Halloween, all spirits like to dance. She came around to seeing it as a way to get on the ghosts' good side.)

"I don't think you should invite Black John and Little Bit, Truman," said Big Boy. "Some people might have a problem being at a party with, you know . . . black people."

"Oh, nonsense! We'll dress 'em up so good, no one will even know it's them! Besides, we have to invite Edison. He can do his choo-choo imitation and we can ride his train from game to game. He'll be the frosting on the cake!" said Truman.

Nelle and Big Boy shrugged. It was Truman's party and he could do whatever he wanted.

35
Inviting the Question

Truman used all his best storytelling techniques to convince Jenny to host the party. She would be the talk of the town, and inviting the most important people in the county would be good for business. Heaven knows, she needed the business, so, for once, she and Truman were on the same page.

Since nothing special ever happened in Monroeville, word quickly spread about Truman's last hurrah. Everyone at school wanted an invite, and even the bully Boss pretended to be nice (by not threatening to knock the steam out of him).

Down at Jenny's shop, people she hadn't seen in months turned up, hinting that they weren't doing anything special on Friday night. Of course, both Truman and Jenny enjoyed being popular and took a certain joy in turning down those who'd been particularly cruel to them in the past. Or if not turning them down, at least making them work for an invitation. When Billy Eugene and the boys offered to help, Truman took the high road, putting them to work setting up. He took a certain glee in bossing them around for once.

Sometimes, all it takes to ruin a party is one bad apple. Boss Henderson was told that he wasn't invited, so he vowed revenge. He overheard Edison happily telling someone down at Mudtown that he had been invited to Truman's party, and he spread the word that some black kids had been invited to the party over him. When he told his daddy, Catfish, the gossip really got going. And when small-town people start to talk, the next thing you know, the sheriff shows up on your front doorstep.

Whenever Queenie barked, trouble was sure to follow. Truman and Nelle heard Queenie raising a ruckus and peeked out from their treehouse just in time to see the sheriff's patrol car pull up. They both remembered their last encounter with him. Truman took out the guest list, which was filled with more than a hundred names, some crossed out. "Did we forget to invite the sheriff?" he asked.

The sheriff growled at Queenie, who turned and hid behind a japonica bush. Miss Jenny came down from the porch wearing a pink cotton dress. It was her day off, and she did not like dealing with unpleasantries on her day off. The sheriff visibly stiffened as she approached.

"Morning, Sheriff. What brings you out today?"

The sheriff removed his hat. "Morning, Miss Jenny." He cleared his throat. "I've heard rumors—rumors I don't necessarily believe, but you know how people are when they get to talking."

"Continue," she said, crossing her arms.

"Well . . . folks say little Truman has plans to show the people of this fine town a thing or two before he heads up north."

"Such as?"

"Well, ma'am, such as . . . inviting coloreds to y'alls party and having them dress up in costume so nobody will be able to tell they're colored until the party's over—and by then it'll be too late."

Jenny could hear Truman giggling in the distance, but she ignored him. "Too late for what?" she said sternly.

Sheriff put his hat back on. "Thing is, this is the kind of situation that gets the Klan all hot and bothered. They're planning a rally on the night of your party. They even told Little Bit to leave the neighborhood and stay in Mudtown this weekend."

Jenny had heard enough. She stepped right

up to the sheriff's face. "You know as well as I do the Klan is just stirring up trouble because they have nothing better to do. Membership is down and they haven't had anything to protest for a while, so why not pick on some little boy's going-away party? Of all the nerve! You tell them if they want to threaten me and my family, they should do it in person and not send their messenger boy!"

The sheriff did not appreciate being lectured by a woman.

"Now, Miss Jenny, I've told them not to interrupt your party, but it might be out of my hands—"

Jenny spun on her heel and headed back in. "Just do your job, Sheriff, or I won't be contributing anything to your next campaign!"

The door slammed. The sheriff shook his head and slowly got back in his car. Before he shut the door, he gazed up at the treehouse for a good five seconds, until Queenie came out from behind the bush and started barking again. He revved his engine and drove away.

"Is the coast clear?" asked Truman.

Nelle was impressed. "Wow, I've never seen Miss Jenny so angry," she whispered. "She must really care about you."

Truman nodded. He was impressed too.

Nelle watched the patrol car turn the corner past the Boulars' house. Her eyes came to rest on Sonny's home. It seemed dark and forbidding even though it was broad daylight.

Nobody had seen or heard from Sonny since that day in the courthouse almost a year ago. It was like he was a ghost who'd just faded from memory.

"I was thinking . . ." she said.

"What about?"

"About . . . Sonny," she said.

Truman grew quiet. He still felt bad about what had happened to him.

"Maybe we should invite him to the party too?" she asked.

Truman almost choked. "I don't think his pa will allow him out of the house to come to a party!"

Nelle shrugged. "He might . . . if we invited his sister too," she said slyly. Sally Boular was a well-liked normal girl who suffered under her brother's reputation.

"Well . . . she's nice and all. Maybe I wouldn't mind if *she* came," said Truman. "But you and I know that just having Sonny Boular show up will scare the pants off everyone."

Nelle smiled. "Well, it *is* a Halloween party—"

A grin slowly spread across Truman's face. "Oooh . . . I hadn't thought of that! It'd be like having a *real* ghost at our Halloween party. Good idea, Nelle."

"That's not exactly what I meant, Truman."

"Yeah, well, it's still good . . ." he said, rubbing his chin.

Nelle continued. "I think he's lonely, trapped in that house. He deserves to get out now and then. 'Specially after what we done."

Truman nodded. "You're right. We'll invite the Boulars." It would be a perfect way to cap off the Halloween party of the century.

36
All Hallows' Eve

Halloween. The night of the party was finally upon them. Sook spent all day preparing molasses candy, little cakes, and punch for everyone. It was the only way to keep her from crying at Truman's farewell. Truman made sure to spend as much time as he could helping her out, just so she wouldn't feel so sad. He helped sift and measure, roll and pour. He kept the fire stoked in Ol' Buckeye and tasted every cake and candy to make sure it was up to her standards.

Stirring the punch for the adults, Sook said, "Tru, honey, never forget how much you mean to me. Just you remember, Sook loves you more than anybody."

He would not forget.

Cousin Bud, as promised, built a ramp off the back porch so the kids could ride the Tri-Motor plane down it. Anything for Truman. Jenny spent considerable time helping Black John White set up lights all around the backyard. Even dreaded Cousin Callie got into the spirit of things and traveled by bus all the way to Montgomery to pick up a special order of bobbing apples that came in from Washington.

Nelle told Truman that, unfortunately, the rest of her family would not be attending. Her sisters were away in Montgomery for a college sorority party, and A.C. would stay home, keeping her mother company, as she was still too fragile for such a large event. Truman understood and promised to save them some cake.

Truman, Nelle, and Big Boy spent all day planning the games for the party. One of their favorites involved three boxes they'd made that each had two holes on one side. People had to stick their hands in and guess what was in there. One box had a squirming green tortoise, another had a pile of mashed-up bananas and oranges. The final one held a duster made of turkey-wing feathers. Other games included Pin the Tail on the Donkey, which Truman had decided would be better with a real donkey. Bud agreed to loan them his donkey, but only if a pin wasn't used.

Nelle and Big Boy painted their faces and wore old oversize clothes so they looked like hoboes. Truman dressed as Fu Manchu, with a long mustache and ponytail made out of hair from one of Bud's ponies. Sook dressed Queenie up in a circus costume that she'd made herself. She couldn't stop laughing at how cute that dog was.

Dusk settled in and the fireflies soon sprinkled the backyard with stardust. It was an unusually warm night for late October. People began to arrive, and Truman and Jenny stood at the front door to greet them. He bowed with his hands pressed together the way he imagined Fu Manchu would, then he checked off people's names, made approving comments on their costumes, and rated them on a clipboard. He liked that Mr. Barnett showed up dressed as a pirate (he had a wooden leg). He was amused when Billy Eugene and his pals showed up dressed as a chain gang. Jenny beamed with pride as the most important members of town all showed up. There were over a hundred people on the list, and it looked like they were all coming.

There were ghosts and devils, knights and dragons, criminals and cowboys, and even a nun (Cousin Callie). The adults listened to Al Jolson records on Jenny's Victrola player, something few people had ever seen or heard before. The children ran wild in the backyard, bobbing for apples or sticking their hands into the mystery boxes or dancing to Little Bit's accordion music (she was dressed as a ghost too). Black John White was having himself a time, jumping out from behind a tree and scaring the kids, then telling them jokes to unscare them. Edison dressed up as a train conductor and shuttled kids from game to game. Billy Eugene behaved. Nelle and Big Boy took turns riding Truman's plane down the ramp, over and over again. Truman seemed pleased.

The party was a big success. Truman stood on the back porch on that warm October night marveling at the crowds of masked kids and adults. Even with the costumes, he knew who everyone was. The only kids that appeared to be missing were the Boulars.

So lovely was the party, no one seemed to notice the line of cars that slowly passed by the house and parked down the street at the school-yard. Men in white robes got out and put hoods over their heads. These were not costumes but the real deal. Torches were passed around and lit. Then they headed slowly toward Truman's party.

Everyone was having a swell time—until someone screamed.

37

Uninvited Guests

Help, please help! The Klan's got Sonny and they're going to hang him!" It was Sonny's sister Sally dressed as a princess and crying her eyes out. She collapsed into Jenny's arms in the living room. "We were on our way over in our costumes but Sonny was lagging behind. When they spotted us, they thought he was following me. They yelled, 'There's one now!' and chased him down. I got scared and ran, but Sonny tripped and fell in front of Mr. Lee's house, and that's where they grabbed him!"

Jenny held the poor girl. "Where's the sheriff?" she demanded. No one knew.

All the adults gathered around the front door or stared out the window at the spectacle of a group of twenty or so men covered in white robes and hoods. "Maybe they're just dressing up for the party?" said someone feebly.

Queenie was running around the yard in circles, barking and acting hysterical. Truman, Nelle, Big Boy, and all the children heard the ruckus and ran to the stone wall to see what was going on. They peered over the top and saw a group of men with torches leaning over something in the road in front of Nelle's house. To Truman, it looked like a bunch of ghosts with dunce hats milling about.

"I'd best go tell A.C. what's going on," said Nelle, concerned. She quickly scrambled over the top and the boys followed. "This looks like another case, Sherlock," whispered Big Boy.

But Truman knew it wasn't. "Hush, Big Boy.

Even Sherlock might not be able to get out of this mess . . ."

They snuck in through Nelle's back door. "A.C.?" Nelle called out.

There was no answer. The house was dark except for a single light coming from her parents' room.

"A.C.?" She peeked in, but the bedroom was empty. "Where are they?"

"Over here," whispered Big Boy.

Nelle and Truman found A.C. in the living room, which was lit only by the torch light coming from the street. He stood, silhouetted in the frame of the open front door, dressed in his undershirt and pajama bottoms.

"A.C.? Where's Mama?" asked Nelle.

"Hiding" was all he said. He motioned for her to stay put, then walked slowly down the front steps toward the mob, careful not to startle anybody.

"A.C.!" Nelle hissed.

Her daddy peered over his shoulder and saw the kids in their costumes. "This isn't the time for fun and games, children. Let me take care of it."

A.C. made his way across the front yard to the fence. It was deadly quiet except for the sounds of the torches burning and the whimpering of a boy.

He waded into the middle of the costumed mob and not a word was spoken. They simply stepped aside.

Nelle couldn't stand it. She followed him out into the street. Truman fretted; he still hated himself for the last time he'd abandoned her.

"Oh, shoot. Stay here, Big Boy. No sense in all of us getting killed."

He made his way across the front yard, his Fu Manchu hair floating behind him. He caught up to Nelle and wrapped his hand around hers. "I'm coming too," he whispered.

She nodded and they both snuck up behind A.C.

Some of the men stared at these bizarrely costumed kids and seemed unsure what was happening. Someone shoved Truman as he passed. He stumbled and looked up to see a gigantic hooded person who sniped, "Nice party, maggot."

Even with the hood, Truman knew it was Boss.

What caught his attention more, though, was the man dressed in green robes blocking their way: the Grand Dragon.

The Grand Dragon stood his ground, his arms crossed. The man's eyes glared at A.C. from deep within his hood. Behind him, on the street, was a messy pile of boxes, all painted silver. Truman noticed the boxes moved, and he spotted two round holes cut out in the box closest to them. He heard a whimper coming from inside it.

Truman and Nelle saw the cardboard cubes were wired together to form a costume: a child-like robot. The robot was struggling to get up but couldn't because the boxes made his arms and legs too stiff to bend.

"Now, A.C., this don't concern you," said the Grand Dragon. "You're a respected man 'round these parts; let's keep it that way."

"Step aside, Mr. Henderson," said A.C.

"It's Catfish," whispered Nelle to Truman.

The Dragon flinched. "This is one of those Negros that boy invited to his party. Do you really want them mingling with your children?"

Truman suddenly realized he had gone too far. To do things differently was one thing. To upset the order of Monroeville was another.

"I do," said Nelle as she stepped in front of A.C.

Truman sighed and also stepped up. "Me too," he said, holding tightly to Nelle's hand. "Plus, it's my party."

"*Our* party," said Big Boy behind them.

Queenie growled at the Grand Dragon from behind Big Boy.

The Grand Dragon glared back at all of them.

"You heard the children," A.C. said.

For a tense moment, they just locked eyes.

Then, without a word, A.C. calmly stepped around the Grand Dragon and reached down to offer a hand to the robot. One of the robot's arms reached up to meet his hand. It was painted black.

"Help me!" the robot whimpered.

A.C. grabbed one arm and Nelle and Truman quickly grabbed the other, and they helped the robot to its feet. A.C. removed the tape and wire that held the cardboard head on.

He finally yanked it off, and there was Sonny Boular, white as a ghost, tears streaming down his face.

38

A Mystery Solved

I didn't mean nobody no harm," he cried. "I just wanted to come to the party like everyone else."

A.C. stared at the torches and the men in their fearsome robes and hoods. "See what you've done? You've scared this boy half to death—all because you let your ignorance blind you. What happens at Truman's party is none of your concern. You all should be ashamed of yourselves."

The adults from the party had streamed out

of the house and now stood behind A.C. in a row of solid support. They were the most important folks in the county—the judge, the bank president, the sawmill owner, the county commissioner, the mayor, and, of course, Jenny, all glaring at the Klan members. Behind them, Edison, Little Bit, and Black John White stood in silence.

The men in robes shuffled their feet until one of them said, "Well, shoot. I'm going home."

The other members mumbled and whispered to one another. One by one, they put their torches out in the dirt and wandered off into the darkness, leaving only the Grand Dragon and Boss behind. Finally, even Catfish threw up his hands. "God will judge you, A.C.," he said, grabbing Boss and pulling him away.

"I'm prepared for that, Mr. Henderson. Are you?" said A.C. as he watched them slink off.

Right before getting into his dad's car, Boss got in the last word, which Truman could barely hear. "I'll get you later, runt," he said.

As the last car drove off, the sound of cicadas

slowly came back. Truman turned to Sonny. "You can still come to my party if you want," he said. "I think your costume is swell. In fact, as judge of the costume contest, I think I'll name yours best costume. Congratulations!"

Sonny sniffed and tried to rub his tears away on one of his cardboard arms but only left black streaks on his face.

"Here, let me," said Nelle. She took a rag from her costume and dried his eyes. "I'll bet you can still bob for apples in that getup. You'll have to keep your robot head off, though . . ."

As Nelle led Sonny inside, something sparkly on the chest of his robot costume caught Truman's eye. At first, Truman thought it was just a costume button, but when he inspected it in the light, he noticed two red stones staring back at him. They were the eyes of a green snake.

Truman nudged Nelle and pointed to the cameo brooch glued to his costume. Nelle smiled and shook her head.

"Say, Sonny," Truman said. "That's some button you got there."

"A snake." He grinned.

"Why do you like snakes so much?" asked Truman.

Sonny stared off into the distance. "When . . . I was eight . . . I had a pet snake. I loved him so much. Then he passed."

Nelle took his hand. "I had a pet rabbit once. A hawk killed him. I was sad for a whole month."

Sonny nodded. "I had to put my snake back in the ground, 'cause that's where snakes live, even when they're dead. But I promised I would never forget him. He was a good snake."

Sonny's whole face seemed to change. He almost looked like a normal young man . . . except for his beaten-up robot costume. His sister came up and helped him into the party. Jenny offered them cookies and punch and complained about the sheriff to the other adults. Many of the partygoers had had enough excitement for one night and slowly said their goodbyes and made their way home.

Someone started playing the piano in the parlor, and Nelle knew right away that her mom had joined the party. Truman had never really seen her before. She was a big woman, but nimble. And could she play! A.C. followed the sound of music and smiled when he saw his wife playing. He sat down next to her and listened to her play for the rest of the night. Despite the early scare, she was in fine spirits; she even played a song for Nelle, "Tea for Two."

Nelle knew all the words.

39
Goodbyes

As the evening wound down, Nelle and Truman watched Big Boy challenge Sonny to a bobbing-for-apples contest. "Well, looks like you got your wish, Tru," said Nelle.

"How's that?" he said, stroking Queenie on his lap.

"You pulled off a party that nobody will ever forget."

He smiled, nudged her in the shoulder. "*We* pulled it off," he said.

Nelle smiled. "Yes, we did."

They stared up at the stars overhead. The music was playing, Little Bit and Sook were dancing a jig on the porch, and Black John White and Bud were resting against a tree, eating cake. Queenie slept like a baby.

"Your daddy's quite something," said Truman. "Did you see him stare down the Grand Dragon? I think there might be a story there."

"Well, what're we gonna do about our typewriter?" she asked. "Now that you're leaving and all."

Truman thought about it. "You keep it. I expect to see that story when I come back for a visit. Besides, my new dad promised to get me one."

Nelle nodded. "Fine, I'll write one story. But then you gotta write two."

"Fine."

He glanced over at the Tri-Motor airplane standing next to them and grew quiet.

"Someday . . . I'll take you away from here, Nelle. Just the two of us," he said solemnly.

"Sure," she said. "We'll go far away, maybe up in the clouds, and just sail around and watch everybody below."

He laughed, running his hands along the green wings. "Maybe we should go on one last trip together before I leave?"

Nelle stepped up next to the plane. "Okay. But where's your plane gonna take us?"

He lowered himself into the cockpit and tested the pedals. "I dunno. If you push me hard enough and jump on in time, I'll bet we can make enough speed to get us to . . . Morocco!"

"You think?"

He shrugged. "We'll never know until we try." He dug out his goggles and cap from his jacket pocket and pulled them onto his head.

Truman held up his finger to test the wind as Nelle steadied herself behind him. "I'm gonna miss you, *Streckfus*," she said.

He shook his head. "I'm gonna miss you more, *Na-il Har-puh!*"

And with that, she gave him the biggest push ever, jumped on the back of Truman's plane, and held on for dear life.

The End

OTHER STORIES

Truman Capote was fond of the short-story format, and many of his books were made up of a longer novella complemented by several short tales. In that spirit, here are some short stories inspired by Truman's and Nelle's adventures back in the day. Unfortunately, none of their short stories survived that period. Rumor has it that Lillie Mae burned them all in a fit of rage.

> *"I want to write about my own life, about what it meant to be a child in the South ... about Jenny and Sook and Bud and the life we all lived together in that big house. About riding on those big steamboats where my father worked. About tap-dancing while Satchmo and his band played. About all that time."* —*Truman Capote*

The Case of Truman's Missing Plane

Truman was so proud of his Ford Tri-Motor airplane. He'd sit in that dumb thing and putter around the yard for hours on end. Me and Big Boy was always pestering him for rides but he would shake his head no as he rode up and down the road. If I gave him a sweet, he'd let me ride it for about ten seconds and then it was "Time's up, Nelle!"

He was always going on about how that thing could actually fly. "It's true. Bud drove me over to North Hills and he pushed me down the biggest hill and I went so fast, by the time I got to the bottom, the plane started to fly!"

Big Boy fell for it. "How far did you fly, Truman?"

"I went up high enough where I could see the whole town spread out under me. I circled the courthouse clock a few times, then flew low enough to scare Mr. Farnsworth's cows before I landed right back here."

"Prove it," I said. "Let's go ask Bud an' see what he says."

"Oh, Bud's sleeping. You know when his asthma gets bad, he needs his rest."

"What was it like, Truman? Can I go flying too?" asked Big Boy.

Truman put his arm around Big Boy. "Someday. It was pretty scary, I have to say. I wouldn't want you to get hurt or anything."

"Well, what about me?" I said. "I ain't scared of nothin'."

Truman winked. "Good things come to those who wait."

Well, me and Big Boy couldn't wait no longer. One day, when Truman went to New Orleans to visit his parents for the last time, we decided to try it ourselves. He kept it in the room he shared with Sook. And we knew Sook always took a nap after lunch.

We snuck in the back door after Little Bit left for the afternoon. I peeked through a crack in the bedroom door and saw Sook taking her medicine. I knew she'd be asleep in a few minutes.

Me and Big Boy waited, then tiptoed in as quiet as mice. There it was, wedged between the two beds, shining like the *Spirit of St. Louis* herself. But Queenie was standing in front of it, staring at us.

I looked at Big Boy. If the dog barked, the jig was up. I went into the kitchen, glanced around, and spotted a bowl of collard greens sitting on the counter. "It's worth a shot," I whispered.

I put the bowl on the ground and motioned Queenie to come over. The dog tilted his head and padded over to the bowl. He took one sniff and started chowing down.

"Well, I'll be," whispered Big Boy. "The dog eats his vegetables."

While Queenie was busy, we snuck into the bedroom. The floor creaked as we tried to pull the plane out, but Sook just turned over on her side.

It must have took us a good ten minutes to

get that plane out the room, down the hall, and outside. I was sure Queenie was going to bark, but he just sat there watching us with a strange look on his face. Maybe the collards didn't agree with the dog.

Once we made it outside, we were delirious with happiness. We rode up and down every sidewalk and hill we could find. After two hours of this, we were plumb tuckered out.

"Now what should we do?" I asked.

Big Boy's eyes lit up. "Let's take it flying!"

I knew it would never get into the air. "We're too far from North Hills to build up enough speed to get flying."

Big Boy was staring straight into the big blue Alabama sky when he got another idea. He pointed over to the roof of Miss Jenny's barn. "If we can get the plane up on the roof, I'll bet we can fly it from there, no problem."

Before I could say anything, he ran into the barn and found a ladder. We set it up against the side of the barn and somehow managed to drag that plane up there, him pulling and me pushing till we plunked it down on the roof. I gazed down at the neighbor's pig yard beside the barn below us. We were pretty high up. "You sure you want to do this?"

"Believe me, once I get airborne, you're gonna want to be next!" he said. He reached into a compartment in the plane and pulled out Truman's goggles. He strapped them on. "Now, Nelle, I want you to give me a big push."

"What about them pigs?" I pointed down.

"What, them? I'm gonna soar right over those hogs and sail down to the pasture over yonder."

"Whatever you say . . ." I shrugged and grabbed the tail of the plane. "You ready?"

He tucked himself into the plane and adjusted his goggles. "As ready and steady as rain."

I gave him the biggest push I could. "Fly, fly, *fly!*" I yelled, hoping he would.

Big Boy and the plane sailed off the edge of the barn, and for a second, he *was* flying. "Woo-hoo!" he yelled.

Then the plane nose-dived into the earth, crashing smack into the muddy pigpen and sending Big Boy flying into the hogs in a wave of watery muck and manure.

"Oh my gosh! Big Boy! Are you all right?"

He was lying face-down in the mud. He barely lifted his head. "Ow."

The hogs were squealing in anger, upset by this invasion. I knew from experience that when they were mad, they bit. Hard. And I'd never seen them this upset before. They were kicking and thrashing at the plane. And one of them had just spotted Big Boy.

"Big Boy, get outta there! Them hogs'll eat you alive!"

The next thing I knew, I had jumped from the roof into the mud myself! My screams sent the hogs squealing. I crawled through the muck to save Big Boy. "Are you still alive?"

He lifted his mud-covered goggles. "I think I'm still in one piece. My arm stings a bit."

We heard some grunting and looked over at the hogs, who were getting ready for another charge. "Hurry! We gotta get out!"

"What about the plane?" he asked.

We both grabbed it on each end and managed to throw it over the fence and climb over before the hogs got us. We collapsed on the grass. Big Boy started laughing.

"Your hair, Nelle! You look like a mud pie!"

I felt my head and came back with a handful of glop. "Ugh. I wouldn't talk, Big Boy," I said, throwing the goop at him.

We both had a good laugh until we inspected Truman's plane. It was smashed, muddied, and broken. It would never fly again. "What're we gonna tell Truman?"

"Let's wash it off as good as we can and put it back."

We pushed it to the barn and cleaned it off. The propeller was gone and the wings bent in all kinds of directions. "Oh, Big Boy . . . Truman's gonna hate us for this," I whimpered.

Big Boy spotted an old rusty pickup truck swerving by the house. He watched it as it nicked a trash can sitting on the curb, sending it spinning into the road. "I think I know what we can do. We can tell a half-truth."

"What's a half-truth?"

He shrugged. "We'll tell him we took the plane out without asking him. Then we got hungry and left it on the curb while we ate lunch. And that's when my uncle Howard smashed into it with his truck."

I was skeptical. "I don't know . . ." I said. "Why your uncle?"

"'Cause he likes to drink. And when he drives after that, he swerves all over the place. We'll just tell Truman that he ran into the curb and smashed up the plane. Uncle Howard won't remember a thing."

I shook my head. "I don't like it, but I guess we got no choice. If he ever knew the truth, he'd disown us."

Well, Big Boy got his comeuppance, even before Truman came back. His arm ached like the dickens that night, and by morning, it had swelled up like a balloon. He had broken it in the fall and now had to wear a cast.

Me, Big Boy, and Big Boy's cast stayed away from Truman for a few days after he returned.

When we finally got up the nerve, we went over to his house. The first thing I saw was that plane lying in a heap of trash. He came out to the gate to see us.

"I'm so sorry, Truman. We shouldn'ta taken it and let it get wrecked like that," said Big Boy.

"Yeah, I'm sorry too, Truman," I said. "Really, I feel so bad."

Truman noticed Big Boy's cast. "What happened to your arm?" he asked.

"Um, I broke it when I fell off the barn." Half-truth. Big Boy was always doing silly things, so Truman didn't even question it. He was too upset over his plane.

"I really liked that plane, more than any present I ever got," he said, looking over at the trash. "I guess there's no such thing as magic anymore."

"Whaddya mean, Tru?" I asked.

"Well, back when Lucky Lindy flew across the Atlantic Ocean all by himself, no one believed he could do it except me and Daddy. The whole trip, we listened on the radio, praying for him to make it, and every time we heard an update, we'd dance in a circle clockwise, snapping our fingers. That was our magic ritual to help him. And he made it, all right. But now, I'm not so sure. Nothing seems to work anymore."

I held his hand. I hated to see him that way. "What if . . . what if we fixed up your plane?"

Big Boy shook his head, but I ignored him. "Bud is good with tools. I bet between him and Black John, they could make it good as new!"

Truman beamed. "You think?"

Big Boy rolled his eyes. "Nelle, don't say that!"

Truman shot him a look. "Why not, Big Boy?"

Big Boy hemmed and hawed, then gave up. "'Cause . . . durn it, *I'm* the one who's gonna fix it, that's why. And Nelle is gonna help me!"

I nodded. "Sure thing, Big Boy. We'll get that plane up and running again, you'll see."

Truman put his arms around us. "That would make me so happy."

Well, later, Black John and Bud took a look

and shook their heads. "It'll be easier to buy a new one, bang it up a bit, and tell him you fixed it."

"But how we gonna pay for that?" I asked.

Bud thought about it. "I'll front you the money, but you two will have to pay it off."

"How?" asked Big Boy.

Bud smiled. "Got twenty acres of cotton coming up for harvest. Was gonna git a bunch of folks from Mudtown to come pull it, chop it, and haul it to the cotton gin. But now I got a better idea . . ."

A month later, Truman had a new old plane. Me and Big Boy had cut-up fingers and bruised backs. It was the last time we'd ever "borrow" from Truman again.

Sook's Secret Recipe

When I first met my cousin Sook, she was already a recluse. "Tru, I'm never gonna leave this house again!" she would say. And mostly she didn't; not for church, not for haircuts, not even to fetch herself some tobacco chaw, which she loved more than anything. No, sir, Sook was a regular hermit.

On Sundays, when everyone went to church, she prayed at home. When she needed something from the market, she sent Little Bit or me. When she needed a haircut, the barber came to the house!

She was shy with everyone but me, Nelle, and Big Boy. She seemed ancient, with her thin gray hair and those big eyes that looked right into mine. Jenny, Callie, and Bud tended to treat her like one of the servants. She cleaned the house, collected eggs from the chickens, scoured the backyard for beans and roots, and worked in the kitchen with Little Bit. And all she got was grief whenever she let me do something the adults thought I shouldn't do, like drink coffee or stay home from school to listen to soap operas on the radio or sit around listening to Sook read the comics out loud instead of letting her attend to her duties. Jenny especially could bring her to tears, saying I wouldn't grow up proper if we kept doing all the things we did together. Sook was a regular Cinderella, except old and superstitious.

Superstitious because of a childhood fever that almost killed her — she was afraid of the night because she thought deadly swamp fevers would float through our windows and take us while we slept. So, during the hottest, most miserable nights, Sook kept the windows and doors sealed shut, even if it felt like an oven in there.

Sook never got paid for her work around the house. But she possessed one thing that no one else had, and it was her only real source of money: a secret recipe for dropsy medicine that cured rheumatism (an old folks' ailment). The secret recipe was handed down to her by her mother, who got it from some traveling gypsies before the Civil War. It was hugely popular, and the making of it every spring was a big undertaking, for which I was her only helper.

While Sook refused to go to town or anywhere else, she did, for this one purpose, wander into the forest behind our house in search of ingredients for her medicine. We'd collect the roots from sourwood trees, iron fillings from old bullets left over from the Civil War (there'd been a big battle there, so there were plenty), and various herbs. But she had two secret ingredients that she told no one about—not even me. She kept those ingredients in an old lock box and hid the key.

Once we'd collected everything, she'd bring out the secret ingredients and dump them in an old black cauldron, but only if I had my eyes closed. Then we'd mix in everything else and boil it over a fire in the backyard for days. As the dark sticky liquid turned to thick molasses, we'd pour it through a strainer into bottles. My job was to keep the fire stoked and the pot stirred.

"The medicine must be strong enough to chase illness from the body. When you can't stand the stench no more, it's ready," she told me.

The awful stuff stank all the way to the town square. It drove Bud and Callie crazy, but Jenny was understanding. "It's the only way she earns her keep."

The black syrup became famous all over the county. People came at all hours of the day and night for her secret concoction. She'd sell it to anyone, colored or white, it didn't matter.

"Sickness knows no color," she'd say.

She acted like a wise old doctor when her patients showed up at the door (black folks had to come in the back way). They would show her their swollen joints or sores and she'd examine them without touching, mulling it over in her gray head. Then she'd disappear into the back room and return with a bottle, from which they were supposed to take one sip a day. She charged them a dollar.

Word spread and she always sold out. I'd count the money and we'd use it to buy ingredients for Sook's special fruitcakes, which she gave out for Christmas to people who deserved them, like the poor and President Roosevelt when he was elected over that scoundrel Hoover.

Spies were a problem. She grew paranoid that everyone was trying to steal her recipe, even Jenny. That might have been one of the reasons she never left home: to protect the secret.

I admit, after my parents split up, I worried for my mother, though she did not for me. When her show-business career didn't take off, I wondered if there was some way I could earn enough money so she wouldn't have to marry some old fool and she could come back for me. Sook and I had so many ideas but they always seemed like schemes Arch would come up with. But one day, we were sitting on the front porch with Nelle and Big Boy playing games, and Sook suddenly stood up with a look of surprise.

"I got it, Truman. I know how you can make enough money so Lillie Mae won't have to remarry."

She took me by the hand and led me down by our secret headquarters, leaving Nelle and Big Boy on the porch to wonder what on earth she was gonna reveal to me that would make me rich. As soon as we were out of earshot, she leaned in and said the magic words: "I'm gonna give you the secret to my recipe. With your smarts, you'll make it the biggest thing in Alabama!"

I couldn't believe it. She explained how she was getting too old for all this work and how she hated that Jenny was always after the recipe so she could retire from the hat shop. She'd much rather I had it and use it to make me and my mother happy.

Now I wish I could tell you what she told

me, dear reader, but alas, I can't. I have been sworn to secrecy for life, and not even Nelle or Big Boy could pry it out of me (though they sure did try).

"Sook gave you the secret, didn't she?" asked Big Boy upon my return.

I glanced over at Sook, who was heading in for her afternoon nap. She didn't say a thing; she trusted me that much. I smiled and said to them, "All I can say is, when I make my fortune, you two will be the first employees I hire!"

They were not impressed.

Unfortunately, the business was shut down before I could take it over. Jenny had tried to secretly patent the miracle formula herself and when word got out to the other local doctors, the health inspector came in and shuttered the service forever.

Archulus Persons Is a Big Fat Liar

Truman would never say it, but his daddy is a scoundrel. I mean to say, he's nice and all when he wants to be, but he's always working some scheme or other. I can never trust him when he says, "Nelle, I need a favor." He's constantly working the angles. And poor Truman was the one always getting ignored.

Every time Arch Persons drove up to the house, it caused a stir. Either he pulled up honking and scaring the chickens in some fancy car with a driver or he snuck in the back way like he was a thief. Truman was always excited to see his daddy, but every time he ended up heartbroken because he was never the focus of his father's attention.

Arch was never boring, I'll give him that. He was always coming up with foolproof plans and crazy ideas that would earn him plenty of dough in as little time as possible. Once, I was sitting on Truman's porch on a rainy afternoon with Big Boy and Truman, all of us rocking on chairs, when a big black Packard roared down the road and came screeching to a halt in front of us. The driver's door opened and out squeezed the biggest man we'd ever seen! He looked like Hercules himself but with dark skin. The man held out an umbrella for Arch and walked him to the porch.

"Morning, kids!" Arch tugged on his Panama hat. He gave no special notice to Truman. "I want y'all to meet Sam. He's gonna be the next boxing champion of the world!"

Sam was huge and had a clean-shaved head, which nobody did in Monroeville at the time. He had hands of stone and big elephant ears. He was all muscle and good-looking too, if I do say so.

"Buon giorno!" he said in a funny accent.

"Sam's from Sicily," Arch said. "I found him in Mobile teaching PE at the community college, if you can believe that. Never did I see a finer specimen. The man's a natural-born fighter. And with me as his manager, we're sure to make a fortune."

No matter that he knew nothing about boxing. "I was thinking, Truman," he asked, "maybe you could be my assistant?"

Truman's eyes lit up. "Can I really?" he said.

"Why, sure, son. And Big Boy and Nelle can help out too. We have to have a real team behind Sam to make this work. And you all can start now by helping to unload the car."

"Does Jenny know you're coming?" I asked.

He ignored my question. "Truman, you're in charge. See that all that workout equipment makes it into the living room. We're gonna change it into a gym!"

Truman stuck his tongue out at me. "See? I'm in charge."

"I don't think Miss Jenny will like seeing her living room turned into a gym," I warned.

"Hush now, Nelle, can't you see he's onto something?" said Truman. "Why, I bet Sam there could beat just about anyone, even Jack

Dempsey himself. I'm sure glad he's a nice guy or I'd be scared." Poor Truman always believed his daddy. Or at least, he wanted to.

Before Jenny came home from work, we had moved all her fine furniture and carpets aside and put in a system of pulleys and weights. Little Bit was so upset, she wouldn't come out of the kitchen. When Jenny finally came home from work, she was shocked and furious at Arch. But somehow, the sight of Sam working out and flexing his muscles and the sound of him talking to her in his Italian accent won her over. Arch promised her that she would see some of the profits too.

Arch said he had to go and make some deals with another promoter to get a big fight going in Monroeville. "We'll hold it in the town square and folks'll pay a dollar to see this man beat any challenger. Plus, there'll be the usual side bets, which I know we'll clean up with. Why, Sam here will be a regular moneymaking machine!"

"How much will *we* get paid?" asked Big Boy.

Truman shot him a look but Arch didn't mind. "I like you, Big Boy. Always getting to the bottom line. Well, if you hold down the fort while I'm away . . . I think a quarter a day would be fair."

"Each?" I asked.

He smiled. "Each. But it won't be easy."

"Don't worry, Father. We won't let you down, will we?" He glared at us all.

Well, every morning around six, Truman, who normally slept late, was up knocking at my window. It was time for Sam's morning run. They all drove in the Packard, and me and Big Boy followed along on our bikes. Truman's job was to hang out the side window with a water bottle while Arch drove next to Sam. Whenever Sam got tired, Arch would honk his horn. "Don't be lazy! You want to be world champ or not?"

Arch would stop at the town square while Sam continued to run around and around till everyone took notice. Arch would then stand on a bench and yell through a megaphone: "See the greatest fighter who ever lived! Come this Saturday to see this legendary boxer in person before he's too famous to see up close!"

Arch was a natural showman, and Sam was a hard worker, but what they didn't count on was the scandal of seeing a colored man running in shorts and, often, no shirt. Many of Monroeville's churchgoing women had never seen a man's bare legs before, and by the second day, the church had started a petition to ban the fight. By the third day, church women were marching in front of the house!

Well, Jenny wouldn't stand for it. She convinced sweet Sam that Arch would never deliver on his promises and offered him bus fare back to his job. The next morning, Sam was gone, and so was Arch's dream.

Arch had already collected money on the promise of the fight, so he had to sneak out of town just to keep his investors from finding out. Poor Truman was beside himself. He'd really thought Sam was going to be Arch's ticket to fame and fortune.

His next act was even bigger than Lazarus himself. The Great Hadjah had almost supernatural powers. He had to be seen to be believed.

A Monster Fish and
the Two-Headed Chicken

It all started down by the river one day when
me and Big Boy were out for a walk. "Truman,
look!" Big Boy said, pointing at a bunch of
fishermen drying their nets and traps on a
tree. They were gathered around a small washtub, arguing over something that was causing
a fuss. So we went over to have a look-see and
there it was: a huge prehistoric catfish. It had a
strange jaw like a swordfish's and appeared to
be otherworldly.

"That is the weirdest-looking fish I have ever
seen," I said. "I'll give you a dollar for it." The
fishermen agreed.

"What in the world are you gonna do with
that thing?" asked Big Boy.

"I have an idea. And we're gonna make lots
of money."

Me and Big Boy waited for the fishermen to
deliver the monster to Jenny's. We were sitting

on the porch when Nelle came up. "What're y'all waitin' for?"

"Truman's gonna make us all rich," said Big Boy.

"Really? How?" asked Nelle.

Just then, the fish arrived on the back of a flatbed truck. Truman pointed. "That's how."

Two fishermen carried the tub over to a small pond Jenny had built for her goldfish. "Put it in there," said Truman.

When Nelle saw what was in the tub, she jumped. "Good golly! What is that thing?"

The fish slid from the washtub into the fishpond and slowly moved around. The other fish darted for cover. "That, Nelle, is the eighth wonder of the world—the dinosaur catfish!"

We all stared at it. It was ugly as sin and nobody had ever seen anything like it. "We'll charge a nickel for anyone who wants to see it," I said. "They'll be lining up!"

Nelle tilted her head, and the sea monster slowed down and came to a stop. "I think it's dead," she finally said.

I poked it with a stick, and the monster rolled over onto its back. "Tarnation! I paid a whole dollar for that."

I sat down and thought for a good long while until it came to me. "I got another idea."

I ran over to the shed and found some wire and an old brick. "Grab that fish, will ya?" I said to Big Boy.

"I ain't touching that thing," he said.

"Well, how'm I gonna stick it with this wire unless you hold it?" I asked.

"I'll do it," said Nelle. Any time she could show up a boy, she was game. She knelt down and paused.

"What'sa matter, scared?" asked Big Boy.

She grimaced and reached in to grab it by the tail. "Eww, it's gross." She spun around and shoved it in Big Boy's face. "Kiss me!"

Big Boy ducked and ran to the other side of the pond to avoid the fish. Nelle laughed, and she and the fish gave chase.

After circling the pond a few times, Nelle

got tired of chasing him. "It smells. What're you gonna do?"

I ran the wire through its innards and back out again, then tied it to the brick. We plopped the whole contraption back into the water, and the fish stayed upright.

"But he ain't moving," said Nelle.

I stuck my hand into the water and caused a little ripple. It looked like the fish was swimming. "Good enough?"

"I don't know. If we're gonna charge money, I think we'll need some other spectacles."

My mind raced. "We can make it into a carnival sideshow! We just need a few more freaky things like we see whenever the carnies pass through."

"Doc Hines got a pickled pig baby in a jar over in his office," said Big Boy.

"Ooh, that'd be perfect," I said. "We can make up a story about it, like how on a full moon it comes back to life and wanders the fields digging up grubs."

Nelle rolled her eyes. "You might as well get a two-headed chicken while you're at it!"

Eureka. "Nelle Harper, that's the best idea you've had yet!"

Nelle made a face. "And just where on earth you plan on finding a two-headed chicken?"

I knew Sook and Little Bit were gonna make chicken for supper tomorrow. "When Little Bit gets her chicken, I'll ask for the head. Then we'll just glue it onto another chicken. It'll be perfect! We'll get Little Bit to play accordion and I'll be the master of ceremonies. I'd say that's a show kids'd pay a dime for!"

"I can see you learned something from your daddy," said Nelle.

"Say, don't Bud keep a Confederate sword from his daddy? We can show that off too," said Big Boy.

"Good idea. He also has a pistol his daddy stole off a Yankee," I said. "This is gonna be a show to remember!"

Two days later, we had everything in place. Making the two-headed chicken required some glue and wire, though the chicken didn't take kindly to its second head. I got Doc to lend the dead baby pig, and Nelle and Big Boy made signs advertising the show and talked it up around town.

On the day of the show, kids were lining up. We were gonna be rich! What I didn't know was that Preacher Blake and his family was going to stop by for a visit. The preacher was a serious man of the cloth and his wife a regular pillar of the community. When Jenny came back to get me and saw what was going on, she threw a fit.

"Truman, did you not remember the preacher and his family were coming over? You have to send your friends home now!"

"But, Jenny, they already paid, and we made good money too!" I said, holding it out for her to see.

Jenny noticed Little Bit dressed up with her accordion. "Little Bit, why aren't you in the kitchen with Sook?"

"I done prepped everything this morning, Miss Jenny. I was just going to play one song and be done with it," she said. "You know, for the kids."

Just then, the preacher and his lovely family wandered through the back door and saw the spectacle before them. He saw one of the signs we'd made. "A carnival? Why, we love a good show, isn't that right, Mrs. Blake?" he said.

Mrs. Blake grimaced through tight lips. "As long as it's a decent show and not like those horrid carnies."

"Why, they just kids," said Little Bit. "It's a innocent little entertainment."

Well, things didn't go quite as planned.

First, the preacher wasn't so pleased about his family being charged a dime per person to see the show. I didn't feel bad, considering how much he makes off us every time we go to church. Business is business, am I right?

Little Bit was doing her thing, pumping the Delta blues through that old accordion and really getting into it. I think Mrs. Blake was a bit miffed by the whole thing, because she grew flustered by the suggestive words of the song. Mr. Blake seemed to be enjoying it, though.

When they got to the fish, I made up a fantastical story of a dinosaur catfish frozen in time that came back from the dead. Only problem was, the fish was clearly dead, because the other fish had started eating it. Mrs. Blake looked horrified, but her children giggled in delight.

I quickly took them to pig baby–two-headed-chicken exhibit. They seemed fascinated by the chicken until Mrs. Blake noticed something. "Is that second head . . . falling off?"

The chicken had been picking at it and now it was hanging at an odd angle. I quickly drew her attention to the pig jar, which was under a towel. "And now for the next wonder—" I said as I pulled off the towel.

Well, Mrs. Blake screamed so loud, it almost popped my eardrum! "They got a dead baby! They got a dead baby!" she cried out.

I tried to calm her down, explaining it was a pig, but she jumped back in fright, knocking over the two-headed-chicken display. "The two-headed chicken escaped!" screamed her son. "Someone catch the two-headed chicken!"

Pandemonium broke loose. In the scramble to catch the chicken, Little Bit got her dress torn to where you could see her undergarments, which caused Mr. Blake to back up into the pointy end of the Confederate sword. He let out a bellow of pain—"Of all that is holy!"—and fell back into the fishpond.

Mrs. Blake almost fainted; she leaned against the bench that held the pig baby, which collapsed, sending the jar crashing to the ground. When Mrs. Blake saw the pig baby roll onto her feet, she fainted for real.

Me and Nelle and Big Boy were standing there gawking when we heard two shots ring out. We ran to the road in front of the house where Sheriff Farrish was standing with a smoking pistol. "Did anyone see that? I just shot a two-headed chicken! I think I hit it in the head, but it just kept going!"

That night, Jenny banned carnivals forever.

The Very First Time
I Ever Laid Eyes on Truman

A.C. used to say to me, "Nelle, Monroeville is home to us. People are born, raised, get married, and die without ever a thought of moving away." That's what made Truman different, I suppose, 'cause he was an outsider from the beginning. He was from a different city in a different state. He talked different, he acted different, and he was different in every way imaginable. But then again, I wasn't like anyone else either; maybe that's why we got along in the end.

The first time I ever laid eyes on Truman, I thought he was some kinda precious china doll. This was a couple years before I ever talked to him, back when he visited Miss Jenny with his folks.

Miss Jenny, being the refined person she is, was always ordering delicate things from faraway places. So here, I thought, was this pretty doll sitting on a wicker chair on her side porch, all dressed up in a little white suit, short pants, and a striped tie. It had fine blond hair that looked white under the sun. It seemed so real, I was thinking of using it to scare my sister Bear.

Then it began to cry.

Miss Jenny and her cousin Lillie Mae were having a big ol' argument—so loud I could hear almost every word they were saying from my house. Just when I thought it couldn't get no worse, that doll suddenly started bawling its little head off. I musta been three at the time, but I can still remember it on account of all the crying. My mama, who hates noise 'cause it makes her all nervous-like, pulled me inside.

"Who was that, Mama?"

"That is Lillie Mae's child!" Lillie Mae lived in New Orleans. Every time she showed up here in Monroeville, she caused a stir. She dressed like a showgirl and if she wasn't getting enough attention, she raised a ruckus until everyone noticed. The way she acted upset Mama and so did her kid's crying. Mama sat down and played the piano as loud as she could just to drown them out. Between the piano, the yelling, and the crying, my ears couldn't take it anymore! I hid in my daddy's office until it quieted down again.

After that day, I didn't see or hear that kid for a long time.

'Bout a year later, a big fancy car with no top pulled up and there was that child again, all dolled up in a little sailor suit. Lillie Mae and her husband dressed real fine too, bouncing out of the car like they owned the world. Miss Jenny did not look happy to see them. Folks just didn't act like big-city people here in Monroeville. Me, I was already wearing overalls and going barefoot all the time. Maybe my mama woulda liked a little china-doll kid instead of a tomboy like me, but I knew she couldn't stand them either.

The adults went inside, leaving this little kid to wander around the backyard all alone. Truth be told, last time I saw this kid, I'd thought it was a girl. Now I wasn't so sure. The kid seemed worried about getting the white shoes dirty. But then the kid saw Miss Jenny's bone fence and froze. I hafta admit, that fence kinda scared me too, 'cause it was made from *real* animal bones. Why Miss Jenny would make a fence out of animal bones I never knew, but I wouldn't go anywhere near that thing.

I remember sitting there watching that little sailor inch up closer and closer to that bone fence. When the kid finally touched it, a big ol' grin appeared. Giggles followed. The kid was petting the bones and kinda wiggling on them when Lillie Mae called from the house: "Tru!"

Tru? What kind of name is that? It did not help me solve the mystery of this child, who was real surprised and kinda slipped and fell across the fence, knocking out a few bones. Well, that was like pulling on a thread—as soon as you undid a few of 'em, a whole row came tumbling down.

The look on that face! The kid panicked and tried to fix it but the more it was meddled with, the more it came undone. I started sniggering myself, and then the kid noticed me laughing. Well, if looks could kill—that kid just stood there glaring at me, hands on hips, lower jaw jutting out like a bulldog's. That just made me laugh even more, 'cause that's just what the kid looked like, a little bulldog with two middle teeth missing.

"Tru!" his mama cried. When she came out and saw the kid's dirty suit, Jenny's prize fence all a mess, and her child sitting there caught in the act, she grew angry. Well, before she could say anything, the kid began shaking like a volcano about to blow—face turning beet red and eyes watering like a dam overflowing during a storm. And that's when a wail came outta that mouth that I bet you could hear all the way from the county courthouse in the town square.

Well, the anger just drained from Lillie Mae's face and she started pampering the kid like royalty, just to stop the crying. I listened to the kid make up some big story—"This little barefoot boy in overalls pushed me into the fence!" the kid said in a peculiar, high-pitched voice.

Then I realized that child was talking about me!

That little shrimp. I ducked down behind a bush and watched through the leaves as Lillie Mae carried her kid back inside. Right before they disappeared into the house, that shrimp stuck out a tongue at me, grinning like I'd been had!

That's when I knew that kid was smarter than most of the children around here.

The Road to Monroeville

For the first years of my life, my father, Archulus Persons Jr., never had a job. We'd been living off Grandmother's money, which was a lot, but he'd spent it all on fancy cars trying to impress my mother. He finally got a real job after living off family money and two-bit schemes all this time. He had to go away for a few weeks, but Mommy didn't want me around without him. She kept on saying, "Truman, you make me feel old. I'm still young and too pretty to be dragged down by the likes of you." The final straw came when she said she was sorry she'd ever met him and even sorrier that she'd had his boy.

My daddy didn't say a thing after that. The next day, he took me with him on his trip.

We showed up at the foot of the Big Muddy—the Mississippi River—and there it stood: a real Mississippi steamship, with a paddle wheel and two high smokestacks right out of *Huck Finn*. Painted on the side, I saw my middle name: Streckfus. As in the Streckfus Steamship Company.

"You were named after these boats, son," Daddy said. "When I told Mr. Streckfus, he hired me on the spot and made me the assistant purser. 'Any Streckfus is family to me,' he said."

The boat ran up and down the Mississippi between New Orleans and St. Louis. Daddy didn't want me sitting around getting into trouble, so being the showman he was, he made up a job for me—I was to wander the deck and tap-dance for people. He'd dress me up in my little sailor outfit and had his trumpet player, a grinning black fellow he called Satchmo, play for me as I tapped my little heart out. The passengers loved me and would even throw money at us!

Even after Daddy took his share, I was pretty rich by the time I got back. We stopped at a gift store to get something for Mommy, but I froze when I saw one of the most amazing things I'd ever seen: there, hanging in the front window of the store, was a green Ford Tri-Motor kid's airplane with a red propeller! It was big enough for me to sit in — kind of an oversize tricycle with wings.

"You can have one present," he said. I was stuck on that plane. It looked as grand as Lucky Lindy's *Spirit of St. Louis.*

"That," I said, pointing.

Well, he said it was too expensive and even after I threw a fit, he still said it was too much.

So I asked for a dog. We went looking for a pet store but it was hot and humid and we couldn't find one for the life of us. So we settled on a hat.

Daddy always wore a big Panama hat and so we found one at a hat store just like Cousin Jenny's store. It had a floppy brim that I could pull down over my eyes like a cool detective. We arrived back in New Orleans, and the second Mommy saw that thing on my head, she let Daddy know she didn't like it one bit. It went against all her fashion rules and she threatened to burn it. But I was crazy for it.

As soon as we got home, we were on the road again, heading straight back to Monroeville, where all Mommy's kin lived, particularly my four distant cousins, who all lived under one roof. The hat came with us.

The whole trip, Mommy and Daddy fought over money. She wanted to live like a queen and he was usually broke because of it. But he always had an idea for the next big thing that would make them rich. This time he was running moonshine from an Indian named Joe who lived just outside of town. I overheard him on the phone saying not to worry, the sheriff would never pull over a family with a little kid.

I asked Mama, "How can Daddy catch the moon's shine and tuck it away in the trunk of our car?" She was livid. My oldest cousin, Sook, sat me on her lap and covered my ears as the biggest argument ever cast a pall over the whole house.

Next thing I knew, Mommy stormed out, followed by Daddy, and they left me all alone. Sook held me all night till I soaked her nightgown so completely she had to change and sleep in a gingham dress.

My cousin Jenny, who was old enough to be my grandmother, was just beside herself. When she saw me in the morning, she told me not to worry. "Your mama doesn't deserve your love."

The next week, Sook was by my side almost every waking hour. I helped her cook; we went for long walks in the woods collecting herbs and wild mushrooms, hid out in the attic cutting out the most beautiful pictures in the magazines so we could decorate our kites with them, and after a particularly good day, she would sit me on her lap and let me sip chicory coffee and eat butter beans as we read the funnies out loud. She always started with *Little Orphan Annie.*

She was my best friend those first horrible months. She always had missions for us to fill up the time — especially in those brutally hot summer months. Cousin Jenny was so sick of the flies coming in off the porch, Sook got her to offer a one-penny bounty for every twenty-five flies we killed. The carnage that followed will long be remembered in fly lore — we made almost thirteen dollars in two weeks, enough to get us into the picture show fifty times with money left over for sweets.

Besides Sook, I didn't have any real friends my age outside of these walls until I met the boy next door, who turned out to be a girl. Her name was Ellen spelled backwards.

AUTHOR'S NOTE

Truman Capote and (Nelle) Harper Lee went on to become two of the most heralded American writers of the twentieth century. Truman's acclaimed works include *Breakfast at Tiffany's*, *The Grass Harp*, *A Christmas Memory*, and *In Cold Blood*—a crime story that reunited him with Nelle in 1959. Until recently, Nelle had published only one book in her lifetime, but *To Kill a Mockingbird* has become an enduring classic that won a Pulitzer Prize and sold more than forty million copies worldwide.

To Kill a Mockingbird and many of Truman's short stories were inspired by their years growing up in the tiny town of Monroeville, Alabama. As Truman's aunt, Mary Ida, once said about him, "He took nuggets of truth,

Truman Capote, age 8

Nelle Harper Lee, 1948 Corolla Yearbook

gave them a new twist, and made them bigger than life." Likewise, many of the events told in this book actually happened, but I've rearranged them into a single story and added more than a few fibs for spice, hopefully making for a flavorful bowl of southern homestyle yarns. One rule of thumb holds true: the more outrageous and unbelievable a scene, the closer it is to real life.

After Truman's big farewell Halloween extravaganza in 1933, he moved to New York to live with his mother, Lillie Mae, and her second husband, Joseph Capote, a Cuban business man, who adopted Truman as his own.

Unfortunately, Truman never got along with either of them and ended up being sent to a series of boarding schools (including a disastrous stint at a military academy). In 1939, they moved briefly to Connecticut, where an English teacher saw talent in Truman's writing and encouraged him to contribute short stories and poetry to the school's literary journal and campus paper.

Throughout his years away, Truman sought refuge in the past, returning every summer to Monroeville, where he resumed having adventures with Nelle and Big Boy. Later, however, as money problems arose from his stepfather's embezzling schemes (to pay for Lillie Mae's extravagant spending), these visits became fewer and far between.

Nelle stayed in Monroeville, becoming an independent and strong-willed young woman. In high school, mentored by an English teacher, she discovered her love of British literature and decided she wanted to become the Jane Austen of southern Alabama. Meanwhile, Truman wrote and wrote, his stories about life in Monroeville providing his only escape from exile. He decided not to go to college, and after a short stint working for *The New Yorker* magazine, Truman started publishing short stories in literary journals, where he began to be recognized for his unusually refined style of writing.

After high school, Nelle went on to study law, but dropped out to pursue writing after Truman published his first book, *Other Voices, Other Rooms,* in 1948. Truman based the novel's tomboy character, Idabel, on Nelle.

The following year, Nelle moved to New

Nelle Harper Lee and Truman Capote
fixing plates in the Deweys' kitchen, 1960

York to pursue her dream and supported herself as an airline reservations agent. Truman was her only friend in the big city. However, he introduced her to a couple, the Browns, who in 1956 offered to support Nelle for an entire year so she could finally write her first book. That novel became *To Kill a Mockingbird*. Nelle based the character of Dill on Truman.

In 1959, before her novel was published, Nelle accompanied Truman to Kansas, where he began working on a new kind of book, a "nonfiction novel" called *In Cold Blood*. With Nelle at his side, it was just like the old days, the two of them teaming up to solve a small-town crime—in this case, murder. "The crime intrigued him, and I'm intrigued with crime—and, boy, I wanted to go. It was deep calling to deep," Nelle remembered.

When Nelle won the Pulitzer Prize in 1961, Truman, frustrated by the lengthy and traumatic nature of his project, grew jealous of her success. Despite her newfound acclaim and riches, Nelle returned to Kansas with Truman three years later for the culmination of his research — the murder trials that would close the case — and his story. She was shocked, though, when his book finally came out in 1966, to see that Truman had downplayed her contribution, acknowledging her substantial assistance as "secretarial help." Their friendship suffered, despite both books becoming defining novels of the 1960s, huge international bestsellers, and acclaimed movies. Truman's book did not win the Pulitzer, as predicted by many.

According to Truman, he never quite recovered from the experience of writing that haunting book, and Nelle, overwhelmed by the media hype and attention over her novel, never wrote another novel. Truman died in 1984 of liver cancer, complicated by years of drinking. Nelle hid from the public eye for most of her post-*Mockingbird* life, and now resides in an assisted living facility in Monroeville. A previously lost manuscript, *Go Set a Watchman*, became her second (and last) novel to revisit her childhood with Truman, a fitting end to one of the greatest backstories in American literature.

"We had to use our own devices in our play, for our entertainment. We didn't have much money. Nobody had any money. We didn't have toys, nothing was done for us, so the result was that we lived in our imagination most of the time. We devised things; we were readers, and we would transfer everything we had seen on the printed page to the backyard in the form of high drama. Did you never play Tarzan when you were a child? Did you never tramp through the jungle or refight the battle of Gettysburg in some form or fashion? We did. Did you never live in a tree house and find the whole world in the branches of a chinaberry tree? We did." — (Nelle) Harper Lee

ACKNOWLEDGMENTS

"The year I began school, Truman and Nelle were knee-deep reading Sherlock Holmes detective books. We three would climb up in Nelle's big treehouse and curl up with books. Truman or Nelle would stop from time to time to read some interesting event aloud. We'd discuss what might happen next in the story and try to guess which character would be the culprit. Sometimes Truman called me 'Inspector.' Nelle was 'Dr. Watson.'" — *Jennings Faulk Carter, a.k.a. Big Boy*

Many writers choose the nonfiction biographical format to tell the story of someone famous. In some cases, that can easily turn into the Wikipedia version of a life lived: facts stated in chronological order. Here, I have chosen a different path: to use fiction to capture the poetic truths of a moment in time between two famous writers, Harper Lee and Truman Capote.

What fascinated me was the idea that these two literary giants had been next-door neighbors growing up in a small town in the middle of the Jim Crow–era Deep South, and that they were both misfits who connected over a shared love of detective stories. When I learned that they sometimes played Sherlock Holmes and Dr. Watson to figure out some of the mysteries of their small town and that some of the incidents in their lives formed the basis for *To Kill a Mockingbird*, the storyteller in me couldn't help himself. The characters, the town, and the era were too rich, too colorful, and too outrageous to be contained by nonfiction. A story was born from real life.

None of this would have been possible without the oral histories of Jennings Faulk Carter (a.k.a. Big Boy), as written by Marianne M. Moates in *Truman Capote's Southern Years*

(University of Alabama Press, 1989), and the wildly eccentric and far-fetched recollections of Marie Rudisill, Truman's favorite aunt, co-written with James C. Simmons and published as *The Southern Haunting of Truman Capote* (Cumberland House, 2000). Biographies of Truman by Gerald Clarke, George Plimpton, and Jack Dunphy, and of Nelle by Charles J. Shields and Kerry Madden, plus numerous articles and interviews, filled out the rest. I am indebted to these works.

An odd thanks goes to the actor Philip Seymour Hoffman, whose tragic death in 2014 set the strange journey of this book in motion. Like many fans, I started rewatching his films after his passing, beginning with his Oscar-winning portrayal of Truman in the film *Capote.* That movie reminded me that Truman and Harper Lee had grown up together as children. Curious, I began Googling their childhoods, and further research revealed a series of wonderfully evocative tales about their life in the Deep South. I was surprised that no one had ever written about their friendship in depth, especially for kids. Their real-life stories were outrageous and funny, sad, and all too human. I was hooked.

A huge thanks goes to Jennifer Fox, my go-to friend and former editor, who is also my good-luck charm. Every one of my stories that she's loved has sold. Her insight is invaluable.

Thanks to the copyeditor Tracy Roe for a terrific job making my manuscript clearer and more readable, and to the illustrator Sarah Watts and the HMH design team for making everything look great. Thanks to Charles J. Shields, Tal Nadan and the Truman Capote Papers at the New York Public Library Archives, and Alan U. Schwartz, the literary executor for the Truman Capote Estate, for their help in securing the images above.

To my agent, Edward Necarsulmer IV, a big thanks for thinking I wasn't crazy for wanting to do this. He too felt the magic and kept on the case until the story found its rightful home. 3-4-3, E!

To Julia Richardson, who at first reluctantly rejected an early draft of the story until we discussed it and found out we were much closer of mind than she'd thought. After a short revision with her input, she and HMH loved it. Her fondness and enthusiasm for the characters matched mine and gave these lovable misfits a perfect home.

As always, most important, my utmost gratitude to my wife, Maggie, and daughter, Zola, who continue to keep me grounded, reminding me daily of what really matters in life. Without them, none of this would happen.

And finally, to Nelle Harper Lee and Truman Capote, for inspiring me and millions of readers out there.

The adventures continue!

In this sequel to *Tru and Nelle,* told over three
Christmases, G. Neri transports readers back to the
1930s to revisit all the beloved characters from before. A powerful story of friendship, *Tru and Nelle:
A Christmas Tale* explores race, what it means to be a
family, and the possibility of miracles.

1
Surprise Visit

Do you think he'll be any taller?" asked Big Boy.

Nelle squinted into the hot Alabama sun. It was a balmy seventy-eight degrees in December. So much for a white Christmas. They'd been standing on the side of the red dirt road from Montgomery for more than an hour. The only sign of life was the buzzards circling overhead.

"Nah. I reckon he'll still be a shrimp," she answered.

Big Boy took off his glasses and wiped the dust from them with his shirtsleeve. "Maybe he'll be all fancy and big-city now," he said absent-mindedly.

Nelle looked at him like he was crazy. "You remember that white suit he used to wear all the time? I think he was the only boy in Monroeville who even *had* a suit!"

Nelle was the kind of ten-year-old girl who wouldn't be caught dead in a dress. She wore her usual tomboy outfit: beat-up overalls and white T-shirt, with bare feet. "Heck, he couldn't be more highfalutin and big-city if he tried," she added, spitting into the dirt and watching it turn burgundy.

Big Boy was a farmer's boy; no matter how many baths he took, he always smelled like cows, something the girls never let him forget. Despite his nickname, he was not overly big for an eleven-year-old.

A red cloud rising from the horizon caught his eye.

They stood and stared at the gathering cloud as it grew closer. It took a few seconds before they could see a black speck causing the red tornado of dust. A minute later the black speck became a fancy black convertible.

"Finally," said Big Boy.

The closer it came, the faster Nelle's heart seemed to beat. It had been over two years since their best friend, Truman, had been ripped from their lives. In the beginning, it seemed like she'd gotten a letter from him at least once a week—stories about high-society life in New York, the endless parties, sightings of famous writers and actors, and skyscrapers tall enough to touch the sun.

Then, as winter gave way to spring, and another fall and winter passed, the stories grew shorter and shorter, until they tapered off altogether. She had not heard a peep from him for the past five months—that is, until his older cousin Jenny received a telegram saying he, his mother, and stepdad were suddenly coming to town for the holidays.

"Maybe we should call him Sherlock. You know, for old times' sake?" asked Big Boy.

Nelle broke into a smile, but it quickly faded. Truman was eleven and had been going to some expensive private school. He was sure to be different. Maybe he wouldn't even remember them. Maybe he'd forgotten all the adventures they'd shared or even the mysteries they'd solved together.

The car came up on them fast. At the wheel was a dark-skinned man in a fancy tan suit, smoking a fat cigar. A woman was asleep in the passenger seat.

"Is that them?" asked Big Boy, excited.

A horn blasted, sending Nelle and Big Boy scrambling to the side of the road. As the car flew past, Nelle caught a glimpse of someone in the back seat, slumped out of sight, his white-blond hair blowing in the wind.

They were swallowed up in a tailwind of dust. "Come on." Nelle spat as they grabbed their bikes and followed in the car's wake.

The automobile eluded them, but Monroeville was just a dusty old hamlet and not so big that they couldn't spot a fancy car like that. As Nelle and Big Boy rode through the town square, shopkeepers were just putting up their Christmas decorations, which was always a funny sight, given that a Monroeville Christmas was never like the snowy ones in the picture shows. A winter heat wave was not uncommon in these parts.

"Maybe we should stop and get a Christmas present for him?" suggested Big Boy.

"First we need to find out why he's really here. Something smells fishy to me," said Nelle.

In front of the hardware store, Nelle spotted Mr. Barnett, who had a wooden leg, holding a plastic snowman and staring off down the road. She followed his gaze right to the fancy car, which was parked smack-dab in front of A.C. Lee's office!

Nelle and Big Boy ditched their bikes by one of the grand oak trees that ran down the center of Alabama Avenue. They made their way through a small group of gawkers surrounding the convertible. Truman was not in the back seat. But somebody had filled in the *New York Times* crossword puzzle with the scribbled scrawl of a child.

Nelle gazed up at the second-floor window of her father's office. "Do you think . . . ?"

Big Boy shrugged. There was only one way to find out.

They tore up the stairs as quietly as they could, pausing in front of the second-floor office door on which was etched these words:

Amasa Coleman Lee
Lawyer
Legislator

Surprise Visit

Financial Manager
Editor at Large

Instead of knocking, Nelle motioned Big Boy toward an unmarked side door, which led to a storage room filled with boxes and cleaning supplies.

"What are we doing here?" whispered Big Boy.

She shushed him and closed the door behind them. They stood in the dark except for a crack of light that emanated from another door in the back of the room.

Nelle headed for the light. "That's A.C.'s office," she whispered.

They tiptoed forward until a voice stopped them dead in their tracks.

"Who does he think he is?" shouted a woman. "To do this around the holidays? That is so typical of him. Ruining it for everyone!"

Nelle looked at Big Boy. That was Truman's mother, Lillie Mae, talking.

"Nina, Nina, don't let him upset you so," said a thickly accented male voice.

"Nina?" whispered Big Boy. Nelle shushed him again so she could hear.

"Mi corazón. He cannot win, he cannot," said the man. "Isn't that right, Mr. A.C.?"

"Is that Tru's dad—I mean, stepdad . . . What's his name? Cuban Joe?" asked Big Boy. "And who's *he* talking about?"

There was a pause. Nelle could hear a light tapping; A.C. always tapped a small pocketknife against a table whenever he was thinking.

Her father spoke slowly and deliberately. "Nothing is ever certain in this world. But a wounded and cornered animal should never be underestimated."

"Then we should do what you do to a rabid dog," hissed Nina. "You put him out of his misery!"

"Nina, *mi amor!*" cried Joe. "I sympathize with your ex-husband. He is wounded because he lost the battle for your heart. Don't you see that all he can do is to try to get back at you? *Óyeme*, listen to me: desperate men do desperate things. His only resort is to take our Truman away from us."

Nelle took a step back and bumped into a box that had an old lamp sitting on top of it. She turned just in time to see the lamp teeter on the edge, and before she could grab it—

Crash!

"What was that?" said Joe.

There was the creak of a chair, the sound of footsteps on the wooden floor, and the rattling of the door handle. Nelle and Big Boy stood frozen like deer in headlights.

The door swung open and the silhouette of A.C. Lee towered over them. "Seems like word has gotten out. Nelle, Big Boy, why don't you join us instead of spying on Mr. and Mrs. Capote from the broom closet."

Nelle's eyes fell on Lillie Mae, who was dressed like a Nina, or what Nelle imagined someone named Nina might look like.

Surprise Visit

She had a sleek bob of a haircut, long lashes, and a shiny dress Nelle thought a woman might wear to a dinner club. Holding her hand was Joe, dark-skinned and built like a boxer, with a barrel chest, but his horn-rim glasses made him look soft and kind.

A.C. cleared his throat. Nelle gave him her saddest puppy-dog-eyed look. "We didn't mean nothing by it, A.C., honest. We didn't mean to spy. We was just curi—"

Her eyes fell on Truman, who was sitting in a chair in the corner, scribbling in a small notebook. He looked up at her. His eyes were just as pale blue as she remembered. He seemed older but somehow smaller than before, his feet not even touching the floor. His blond hair was longer and whiter, if that was possible, and he was dressed in a simple suit with tennis shoes.

"Hiya—" she started to say.

Lillie Mae cut her off. "Great! Now *everyone* is going to know," she said, rising from her seat. "These two cannot be trusted."

"But—" said Big Boy.

"Nina, they are just children looking for their friend," said Joe. "They won't say a word. The custody hearing will be but a simple matter that no one needs to know about. Right, kids?"

"Yes, sir," they both answered while staring at Truman.

Nelle had to ask: "Does that mean you're going to live with your dad—with Arch Persons?"

Before Truman could answer, Lillie Mae growled through her dark red lipstick, "If I hear that you two have been gossiping—"

A.C. cut in and ushered Nelle and Big Boy toward the office door. "Perhaps it's best if you go. You can catch up with Truman back at the house," he said.

"But . . . Tru—" Nelle said, looking over her shoulder. Truman just watched as A.C. gently pushed them into the hallway.

"And not a word to anyone," said A.C. before closing the door in their faces.

Nelle and Big Boy looked at each other.

"Boy, she is the most uptight person I ever met," said Nelle.

"Why does he call her Nina?" said Big Boy. "Did you see the way they dressed? All high-society and the like. Joe must be loaded."

Nelle snapped her fingers. "Maybe Arch is trying to kidnap Truman for ransom. I hear he's lost everything," she said.

"I can still hear you," said A.C. on the other side of the door. "Go home. *Now*."

Nelle sighed as she and Big Boy turned and headed slowly out into the sunlight.

On the way home, they paused in front of Cousin Jenny's house. Nelle could see that preparations had been under way all morning in anticipation of Truman's return. They'd broken out the Christmas decorations earlier than usual, since they knew Truman loved the holidays. Nelle could smell the delectable scent of Sook's lemon meringue pie, Tru's favorite, coming from the kitchen. But she and Big Boy needed to talk about what they'd heard back at A.C.'s. And there was only one place for secret discussions: the treehouse.

Since Truman left, the treehouse in the double chinaberry tree that divided their properties had not seen much use. Big Boy lived on a farm out on Drewry Road, and without Truman around, he rarely came over to see Nelle, who was clearly becoming a young woman, despite her best efforts not to.

They snuck past Jenny's house and made their way up the ladder, Big Boy first. When he poked his head up through the escape hatch, he stopped in his tracks.

"Hey, Big Boy. Take your sweet time, why don'tcha?" said Nelle. "I can't hang around here all day, you know."

"Um . . ."

Nelle saw Big Boy glance down at her nervously.

She stiffened. "Is it a snake?"

When Arch Persons's head came into view, she saw that she was partially right.

"What're *you* doing here?" she said. "Can't you read?" She pointed to the No Adults Allowed sign posted by the entrance.

"*Ho, ho, ho!* Good to see you too," Arch said. "Now get your behinds up here before anyone spots you." Big Boy squeezed by him and Arch extended his hand to Nelle.

"I can make my own way, thank you very much," she growled.

When she came up into the fort, Arch was peering at Jenny's house through a cutout window. "They're still at A.C.'s office," said Big Boy.

"So you know, then," said Arch, as if some big secret had

been revealed. He looked silly, a large man in an old suit and cheap glasses scrunched up in a kids' treehouse.

"You hiding from the law again?" said Nelle, suspicious. "I thought you were headed to prison."

"Those charges were all hat and no cattle, for Pete's sake," said Arch. "I'm a churchgoing man now, I'll have you know."

"Uh-huh . . ." Nelle wasn't buying it. "Look, we don't know nothing and ain't interested in any scheme you got cooking up in that head o' yours."

Big Boy cleared his throat. "Well, except that Nina was all upset that you was trying to take Truman from her and all—"

Arch beamed. "Really? You heard that? Serves 'Nina' right."

Nelle stared daggers at Big Boy.

"Just calm down, honey. I'm here to give you an early Christmas present, so give the theatrics a rest, will ya?" Arch said, trying to find a comfortable position to squat in. "You *do* want Truman back, don'tcha?"

Big Boy glanced at Nelle, who tried to contain herself. "What do you mean?" she asked cautiously.

Arch knew he'd gotten her attention. "I mean, if Truman plays his cards right, he could be back to live at his cousin Jenny's by the end of the week, and I mean for *good*."

Nelle stared at him closely. She knew better than to trust Arch Persons. There was no scheme he didn't like as long as there was something in it for him. "What's he gotta do?"

He sighed, as if it pained him to say. "Look, you both know as well as I do that his mother doesn't really care for him. She's a treacherous woman who's just using Truman as a pawn to get back at me," said Arch. "Well, I'm sick and tired of that boy getting used. I'm not trying to get custody. She's got me on that count. But if I win, I might be able to—" He paused, looked around dramatically, then whispered, "Look, I've been talking to the judge, and he agrees that living at Jenny's, surrounded by his elder cousins, would be best for the boy. So if I win, I'd do what's best for him."

"You mean . . . you'd have him move back here forever?" asked Big Boy.

Arch nodded. "If I can put Truman on the stand at the hearing tomorrow and he gets going about the fast life they all live up there in New York, with all the parties, gambling, and drinking and who knows what else—any judge in his right mind would see Lillie Mae for what she is: a sinner who married a gambling, dark-skinned foreigner for his money, for Pete's sake. She's an irresponsible child who needs to be stopped."

Big Boy's mind was racing. "So what do you want *us* to do?" he asked.

Arch smiled softly. "Talk to Truman. Get him to see that what they're promising him ain't on the level, that he'd be much better off here with Sook and Queenie and you two mutts."

"What's she promising him?" asked Nelle. But a car started honking and they all peered out the window just in time to see Joe pulling up to Jenny's house.

"Good, they're here," said Arch. "Look at 'em. Their money offends me. People are suffering in this town and they act like it's still the Roaring Twenties. They've got plenty of dough, but they come after *me* for child support? It ain't right." Nelle could see his face turning red.

His voice dropped and got real serious. "Now get down there and start asking him about all the scandalous things they do up there in the big city. I know how Truman loves spicing up stories to entertain folks. That's all he's gotta do. Perform for a crowd. Sell it like he's being brought up in an immoral way."

"Is he?" asked Nelle.

Arch leaned forward. "They don't call it the Big Apple for nothing. It's the place of the original sin. I heard those two have dealings with gangsters and all kinds of nefarious people. Believe me, the big city is no place to raise a boy as delicate as Truman."